WHOLE LATTE MAGIC

ENCHANTED ENCLAVE MYSTERY #2

SAMANTHA SILVER

CHAPTER 1

I was fairly certain I was going to die.

"I can't do this," I groaned to my cousin Leanne next to me. Every muscle in my body felt like it was about to shut down. There was nothing I wanted more than to curl up into a little ball on the ground and weep until everything stopped hurting.

"You can, you're almost there," Leanne said to me with a wink. Even though she was in the same position as I was, there was nothing similar about the two of us. Leanne was lithe and flexible, looking like she wasn't doing anything more difficult than sitting on the ground reading a book.

Meanwhile I looked like a sweaty bagel.

"And from here we're going to go back into downward dog," Janice said in her relaxing voice from the front of the room."

"Oh, thank God," I muttered to myself. I never in a million years thought I was going to say that; just half an hour earlier I had gone into downward dog and thought I was never going to get out of it.

"See? You made it," Leanne whispered to me.

That might have been true, but at what cost? My left arm was now trembling uncontrollably, sweat fell from my forehead onto the mat below, and I didn't know my quads could hurt this much. I probably would have welcomed amputation if it was offered to me right about now.

"Now, move your knees to the mat, and we're going to go deep into child's pose," Janice said, her voice soft but powerful, echoing through the space of the yoga studio. I looked up and copied Janice, moving my butt back onto my ankles and laying my forehead down on the mat, arms outstretched.

Now *this* was the sort of thing I thought yoga was going to be. Lying on a mat, stretched out, not working every muscle in my body to death.

I could lie here like this all day. In fact, I figured there was a good chance I was going to have to. I wasn't a hundred percent sure I was going to be able to get up from this position.

"Keep breathing everyone. Big, deep breaths. As you exhale, let the stress from the day flow out of you with your breath. Relax your muscles. Relax your body."

I was so relaxed right now I was ready to bite somebody. I wasn't sure my body was physically capable of relaxing anymore.

"And we'll finish off with an 'ohm'," Janice said. The whole room was filled with the low sound of people doing an 'ohm' sound together, the volume slowly rising before fading away once more.

Personally, my sound was more like an "arrrrgghgh-hhhhhhh" but hey, baby steps.

Then, it was over. The other women – and two men – in the room began curling up their yoga mats, drinking water, and happily going on their merry way, looking like models right out of a fitness ad.

I, on the other hand, keeled over onto my side, panting and groaning like a hippo that had just given birth.

"See? You survived. Wasn't it fun?" Leanne asked next to me.

"If masochism is something you're into, sure," I replied. "Please just leave me here. I don't think I can make it to the car."

Leanne laughed, bent down with surprising ease and handed me her water bottle.

"Come on. Drink some water, you'll feel better."

"Is there morphine in it?" I asked, taking the bottle and helping myself to a large swig.

"There isn't. Don't you think you're overreacting just a little bit?"

"No. How was this so easy for you?"

"Because it's not apparently the first time in my entire life that I've exercised."

I glared at my cousin. "Hey, I had to do P.E. when I was in school."

"Right. I bet you were the girl who pretended to get her period so she didn't have to."

I had no comeback to that; it was completely true.

"That's because if this is how exercise feels, I want none of it."

"Trust me, it gets easier."

"I'm going to have to trust you; I have no intention of finding out on my own."

"Wrong," Leanne said. "After seeing you struggle, you are absolutely joining me for the afternoon easy relaxation session in a few days."

"There was nothing easy or relaxing about the last hour. Did you accidentally take me to the advanced, murder-your-muscles session instead?"

"I most definitely did not," Leanne replied. "But we can work our way up to that. You don't have any muscles right now."

"The searing pain every inch of my body is feeling disagrees."

"Alright, well, you're going to have to struggle through it and get up, otherwise the people coming in for the next class are going to see you lying here like a beached whale."

I shot Leanne a look. "A sexy beached whale," she added quickly.

"Fine, help me up," I begged, and Leanne grabbed my hands and dragged me up to my feet.

I picked my mat up off the ground and rolled it up as Janice made her way over, smiling.

"What did you think of your first session?"

"It was great," I lied. Janice was a very nice person and absolutely loved the practice of yoga. I didn't want to break her heart by letting her know I'd rather stab myself than to attend a second class.

"Fantastic," Janet said, beaming at me, putting her hands together, and bowing. "I hope to see you again. Namaste."

"I'm going to nama-stay away from this place in the future," I muttered as she left, and Leanne laughed.

"Oh don't be such a baby. Take a few days to recover, and then we'll come back here again Friday after work."

"I'm moving back in with your mom. She never made me do any exercise."

"She's way less fun than Kaillie and I are, though."

"I don't know; if this is what you consider fun, I'm going to have to disagree."

"Come on. Kaillie's going to be waiting for us, and dinner's going to be cold if we're late. She said she's making shepherd's pie."

If anything was going to make me move right now, it was the promise of food.

The two of us made our way down to Leanne's car, parked on Main Street here in Enchanted Enclave. I'd recently moved in with Leanne and Kaillie, which I did have to admit was a lot of fun. Kaillie was teaching me all sorts of spells, and I was starting to get used to this idea of having magic in my life.

Whereas Aunt Debbie, Kaillie's mom, was all about structured learning and a sort of home-schooling environment, Kaillie and Leanne were much more hands-on. It also helped that Leanne didn't have any magical powers of her own, and so was essentially living vicariously through my discovery of my own powers.

"Hey, Eliza, see if you can turn this bread into toast through magic," Kaillie would tell me in the morning.

Leanne's methods were more... hands on.

"Quick, catch," Leanne would call out in the morning, throwing a plate towards me. The first time it happened, I let out a squeal and ducked – have I mentioned that I'm not the most athletic person in the world – and the plate hit the wall behind me and shattered. "Well, I guess you're just going to have to use magic to fix it."

I'd laugh and cast the fixing spell – one of the first ones I'd learned – and move on with life.

It was a lot of fun, and as I slipped into the passenger seat, I reflected on the fact that I really felt, for the first time in my life, like I had a nice, big, happy family.

It would have been better with Dad here to enjoy it with me, but for me, this was very much a case of a door closing and a window opening in its stead. Things weren't better or worse than when Dad was around, they were just different. And I was enjoying every minute of it.

Leanne was driving back home, where Kaillie was baking up a mean shepherd's pie, when I spotted something out of the corner of my eye. It was a person, walking down the street. No, stumbling down the street would have been a more accurate description. It was dark out, with no streetlights around, and I barely saw them.

"Look out," I said to Leanne motioning in that direction. There were a lot of people here who didn't seem to understand that dark clothing combined with a lack of lights made them practically invisible. Someone must have had a few too many drinks at the bar that night.

"Thanks," Leanne said, slowing down as she moved towards the shape. Suddenly, right as Leanne's car came close to the person, they jumped directly in front of us.

"What the-?" Leanne shouted as she swerved hard, tires squealing to avoid the person. The thud on the side of the car told me that no, she hadn't.

"Oh my God! Oh my God, I just hit someone," Leanne said, slamming on the brakes. "What do I do? What do I do?"

"Stop the car and let's see if they're ok," I said,

unclipping my seatbelt and throwing open the passenger door. I rushed out to see the prone figure lying on the ground. They weren't moving at all.

"Are you ok?" I called out. "Leanne, call an ambulance!"

"On it," my cousin replied, her voice shaking.

I pulled out my phone and turned the flashlight on the person lying on the ground. They didn't seem to be responding at all, which was strange. After all, while Leanne had hit them, it would have been a glancing blow at best, and at slow speed. I couldn't imagine it had done that much damage. But then, what did I know?

Turning on the flashlight revealed that I was looking at a woman who looked to be in her late thirties. She was barely conscious, and her breathing was shallow and ragged.

"You might want to tell that ambulance it's a real emergency," I called out, taking the woman's hand. I didn't know a lot about first aid, but I did know that you weren't supposed to move somebody who might have a neck or back injury, and given as she'd just been hit by Leanne's car, I didn't know what was wrong with her.

"Save me," a weak voice whispered, and I squeezed her hand harder.

"The ambulance is on its way, I promise," I said. "You're going to be fine." I really hoped I wasn't lying to her. The woman tried to move, but I stopped her. "No, stay still. Help is coming."

Leanne came over now, her phone light on as well. As soon as she lit up the scene I gasped.

The woman's shirt was covered in blood.

CHAPTER 2

"*T*hat… that can't be from me, can it?" Leanne asked, any color that had been left in her face disappearing completely.

"No, I don't think so," I replied. It had soaked through her shirt; there was obviously a previous injury there.

"What happened to you?" I asked the woman, but she had passed out, brown curls falling across her face.

I didn't let go of her hand, but Leanne carefully took the hem of her shirt and pulled it up. I gasped as a wound about three inches wide was revealed, right through the abdomen.

"Someone stabbed her," Leanne called out. "Holy crap, Eliza. Someone stabbed her."

Before I had a chance to react, headlights flew into view and an ambulance stopped in front of us a second later. Leanne called out, waving her hands at them.

"She's been stabbed. She seriously needs medical attention, now." The EMTs sprang into action and Leanne and I stepped back as they worked.

"Do you know who she is?" I asked Leanne, and she nodded.

"Yeah. She's a customer at the coffee shop. Her name is Karen. She works as a teacher at the school, little kids. Maybe grade two or three?"

"Why would anyone want to stab a teacher?" I asked, and Leanne shrugged.

"Beats me. Do you think she's going to be ok?"

"I don't know," I replied as they loaded her up onto the stretcher. "It definitely didn't look good."

"I hope I didn't make it worse," Leanne said.

"Hey, don't beat yourself up. For one thing, there was nothing you could have done. She literally jumped in front of your car. You can't expect pedestrians to do that, and as soon as you saw you swerved and slammed on the brakes. Secondly, if you hadn't hit her, we probably wouldn't have stopped and she'd be out here bleeding to death on the street."

"Yeah, that is a good point," Leanne conceded. "Still, I wish I'd noticed without hitting her. What if I made it worse? What if I broke her leg, or something?"

"You didn't do any worse than the person who stabbed her in the first place," I said firmly.

"I guess. But still… I hit her with my car. I can't have made things better."

"Come on," I said. "Here comes a police officer. We

just have to tell them what happened, and then we'll head home."

My heart skipped a beat when I saw who had been sent from the police station – Detective Ross Andrews, the detective with the friendly smile and dimples, eyes that twinkled, and the face of an Adonis. Leanne and I watched as he spoke with one of the EMTs for about ten seconds as the man jumped into the back of the ambulance with the stretcher and drove off, sirens wailing.

"Are you two alright?" Detective Andrews asked. Thankfully, he had left the lights of his car on, so we could still see. Concern was written all over his face, and I nodded.

"Yeah. Just a little shaken up. We weren't expecting what had happened."

"Can you walk me through it?"

"She was stabbed!" Leanne said. "Someone stabbed her."

"Stabbed who? Do you know who it was?"

"Karen. I don't know her last name. The one who teaches at the elementary school. It was definitely her. She ran out at the car, and I tried to avoid her, but it didn't work and I hit her. Oh God, I hit her!"

"Alright, let's take some deep breaths together, ok?" Detective Andrews said.

"Yeah, do one of those 'ohm' things Janice made us do at yoga," I suggested. "She says it's supposed to calm you down and make you feel centered."

"Yeah, well, Janice probably hasn't hit anyone with her car recently," Leanne shot back. "I'm pretty sure breathing isn't going to help Karen."

"Neither is freaking out about it here," I replied. "Come on. Do what Detective Andrews said. Deep breath in, then deep breath out."

After a couple of minutes Leanne was obviously feeling a lot better, and Detective Andrews turned to me. "Do you want to fill me in on what happened next?"

I nodded, trying to forget the image of Karen lying in the middle of the road. "I thought she was drunk. She was stumbling around along the edge of the road, and then all of a sudden she just ran out in front of Leanne's car. In retrospect, I think she might have been trying to get us to help her. Leanne swerved, but still glanced her. We stopped and I ran out, and she was lying on the road, not moving. I didn't want to move her, in case she'd been injured, but she woke up and told me to save her. I said she was going to be fine. Then Leanne came over and we saw the blood. Leanne pulled up her shirt; she'd definitely been stabbed."

Detective Andrews' face didn't betray any emotions. "You say she was stabbed?"

"Well, I'm not an expert, but that's what it looked like, anyway. She had a gash in her side about this big, and blood all over her shirt," I said, showing the size of the wound by holding up two fingers.

"Did she say anything else? Did she mention who had stabbed her, or how it had happened?"

I shook my head. "She just asked me to help her, and then I think she passed out. She was barely conscious when we got to her to begin with."

"Did you see anybody else around as you drove?"

"I didn't," I said, turning to Leanne, but she shook her head as well.

"No, me neither. Seven o'clock isn't exactly rush hour here."

"Ok. I think that's all I need for now. Leanne, I wouldn't worry too much about facing any charges for having hit her. It sounds like there was nothing you could do, and if it really was just a glancing blow, well, it's unlikely charges will be filed."

"Did the EMT say if she's going to make it?" I asked in a quiet voice.

"He didn't look hopeful, let's put it that way," Detective Andrews replied, his face somber. The sound of helicopter blades came from above us.

"That's going to be her," Leanne said flatly. Because Enchanted Enclave was an island, and the hospital here didn't have full-scale emergency services available, anyone who needed emergency care was airlifted to Seattle. There was a helicopter on standby at all times just in case.

I really hoped that in this case, she got there in time.

"Look on the bright side, it means she can't have died yet," I said.

"That's right," Detective Andrews replied. "Alright, that's all for now. Thanks."

"Can you drive the rest of the way?" Leanne asked. "I'm just not sure I'm up to it."

"Sure," I replied as the two of us made our way back into her car. We were less than half a mile from home, but I could absolutely understand her reluctance.

We made our way into the house a moment later to the wonderful aroma of rosemary, thyme and cooked shepherd's pie.

"Took you guys long enough," Kaillie said as soon as we walked in, a wooden spoon on her hip. She looked amazingly like her mother.

"Sorry we're late," I said. "Karen, the schoolteacher, was stabbed and we found her in the street."

Kaillie's mouth dropped open. "Is she ok? Is that what the helicopter was that passed by a couple minutes ago?"

Leanne nodded. "Yeah. We don't know if she's going to be ok. It doesn't look good."

"Oh, geez. Well, dinner's ready and waiting for you. Why don't we eat in front of the TV? I'm guessing neither one of you is up for a good, long conversation."

Kaillie's instincts were right, and despite the fact that it was delicious I mostly just pushed the food around on my plate, and couldn't help but notice Leanne doing the same. I barely even registered the fact that there was a show on the TV; the only thing I could think about was Karen. Was she going to be ok?

"I want to know what happened," Leanne finally said. "Who stabbed her? How did she get to the point where she thought getting hit by my car was the best idea for survival?"

"I want to know if magic could have saved her," I said, looking over at Kaillie. "If I was a better witch, would I have been able to cast a spell or something that could have saved her life?"

Kaillie shook her head. "It's extremely unlikely. I've been told that in the paranormal world there are magical doctors who do have recipes for extremely advanced potions and spells that can help fix paranormals, but we don't know any of those. Being a paranormal world doctor is apparently super hard and prestigious, kind of like here, where they do years of extra training. So no, I don't think even Mom or Aunt Lucy or Uncle Bob would have been able to help. And I certainly wouldn't have. Even if you'd grown up with us, your skills would probably be similar to mine."

"Well, that's a bit of a relief, at least. I would have felt absolutely awful if my magic could have done something to save her and I just didn't know how to use it."

"Don't forget, even if you could, you're not supposed to show any of the humans your magical powers," Kaillie warned. "We have to set a good example and show that we're not the terrible witches the paranormal world seems to think our family is."

I nodded. "Yeah, there wouldn't have been any risk of that. She was basically unconscious."

"I hope she makes it," Kaillie said quietly at those words.

So did I.

CHAPTER 3

The next morning at the coffee shop, Cackling Witch Coffee, Karen's stabbing was the only thing anyone was talking about. Apparently, the news had made it into the Enchanted Enclave rumor mill, since even Janice, who was almost always our first customer of the day, dove straight into it.

"I heard you two were the ones who found Karen last night," she said in a hushed whisper when she came to the counter, even though there was no one else in the shop. "How are you holding up?"

"Alright, thanks," I replied. "I hope Karen will be alright."

"Me too. It couldn't have been easy coming across a scene like that. I wonder what happened to her." Suddenly, Janice's hands flew to her mouth. "Oh my, I didn't make the connection until just now, but it must have happened on your way home from yoga last night."

I stretched my back involuntarily at the mention of yoga. Every muscle in my body was still sore, despite the fact that I had popped a couple of Advil as soon as I woke up that morning.

Of course, Cleopawtra, my cat familiar, didn't understand what was so hard about it and had zero sympathy for my complaining. It wasn't fair that cats were naturally strong and flexible.

"Yes, we were driving back from the studio when it happened," Leanne said. "You haven't gotten any updates on Karen's condition, have you?"

Janice shook her head. "No. I can't believe someone would have done that to such a nice woman. Well, I'll leave you to things. Please take care of yourselves. These things can be very traumatic for everyone, and if you feel as though you need help, do ask for it."

"Thank you, Janice," I said with an appreciative smile. It was nice of her to look out for me and Leanne, as well as showing concern for Karen.

"Well, it sounds like everyone in town has already heard about what happened," I said.

"Just be glad the information is more-or-less accurate," Leanne said. "That's not always the case. A few years ago James Goodrow was overheard in a café ranting to a friend. He told the friend he was sick of his life, because he was dealing with a couple chronic health issues. Someone thought he said he was sick of his *wife*, and there were rumors going around for weeks that they were going to get divorced. Of course, they never did, and James' health issues were thankfully solved."

"Yikes," I replied with a grimace. "Thankfully that story had a happy ending."

"Yeah. James and his wife Denise tell it all the time, they think it's hilarious."

The door opened just then, and I got ready to greet another customer. However, when I saw who it was, I had to work hard to keep the smile plastered on my face.

It was Ariadne Stewart, the woman who owned one of the gift shops here on the island, and who hated – and I meant *hated* – Aunt Lucy.

"Hi there, Ariadne," I said with a faux perkiness that sounded disgustingly sweet even to me. "What can I get for you?"

"I just wanted to see if it was true," Ariadne said, crossing her arms. "I've been told your cousin here hit poor Karen Johnson with her car, and that she hasn't been arrested. That's an absolute travesty."

"The travesty is you daring to believe everything you hear in town," Leanne replied without moving her eyes away from the coffee machine. "Now, are you going to order something, or did you just come here to harass the staff?"

Ariadne narrowed her eyes at Leanne. "I don't know what you did, but I'm sure you belong in jail. I trust the person who gave me this information more than I trust you."

"Well, it's not up to me, either way," Leanne replied. "Besides, what do you think I did, bribed the cops with a hundred? That's not the sort of thing that works around here."

Ariadne crossed her arms and glared at Leanne. "Who knows what someone like you would be willing to stoop to in order to get away with something? Your whole family is crooked. I can't believe you hit that poor woman with your car."

"Well, you're ignoring the part where we probably also saved her life, but hey, I can understand you not wanting to focus on that part," Leanne replied. "Now either order a coffee or get out of here. You're trespassing."

Ariadne glared at us again, then turned on her heel and stormed out of the shop, just as Aunt Debbie came out from the kitchen area carrying a tray full of freshly-baked cookies.

"I highly recommend trying these," she said. "They're raspberry and white chocolate chip, a new recipe Kaillie found online. I think they've come out wonderfully, although I was thinking they might be a better permanent menu fixture in the winter when the weather gets colder."

Leanne and I both went over and grabbed a cookie, still warm from the oven. I bit into it and closed my eyes involuntarily. The tartness of the raspberry mingled with the delicious sweetness of the white chocolate, all enveloped in a spongy, soft cookie.

"Oh, yum," I said. "I disagree. I think these should be on the menu year-round. This is maybe the best cookie I've ever had."

"I'm with Eliza on this one," Leanne replied. "My compliments to the chef."

Aunt Debbie laughed. "Alright, well, I'll keep that in mind. Kaillie and I are working to come up with more of a summer menu now that the weather's getting warmer."

"Still just baked goods?" I asked, and Aunt Debbie nodded.

"Yes. We considered getting some pre-packaged lunch foods and that sort of thing, but we were never happy with the quality, and Kaillie doesn't have the time to make savory as well as the sweets we need for the day. I'm not sure we'd sell enough of them to warrant hiring a second person for the kitchen, as well."

"Yeah, there are too many good places for a quick lunch in town already," Leanne agreed. "I think we're better off focusing on what we do best, which is coffee."

"Right," I said. "Well, either way, those cookies are definitely a winner."

"Thank you," Aunt Debbie said with a smile. She moved to put them in one of the display jars while I bussed a couple of tables, waiting for the next customers to come by. When I got back to the counter, Leanne was staring into space, which was something I rarely saw her do.

"Hey, Earth to Leanne," I said, waving a hand in front of her face. "Are you ok?"

"Yeah," she replied, but her voice betrayed the lie.

"Hey, don't listen to Ariadne, ok?" I said. "You know she's wrong, right?"

"I guess," Leanne said with a shrug. "I wonder how many other people are out there thinking the same thing though. What if everyone thinks I belong in jail?"

"Well, let those people think what they want," I replied firmly. "Trust me. I went through this just a couple of months ago when Leonard was killed, remember? Everyone in town thought I was a murderer. If there's one thing I learned from that, it's that you can't let what other people think dictate your life. Especially not people like Ariadne. She's nasty, and she wants to get under your skin. Don't let her."

"You're right," Leanne said. "Still, I'd feel a lot better about things if I knew more about Karen's condition, and how much damage I actually caused. I really hope she's going to be ok."

"Does she have any family?"

"Yeah, a husband and three kids," Leanne replied. "They're triplets. When they were babies she used to bring them into the shop with her all the time while she downed a triple strength latte."

I laughed. "Wow, no kidding. I'd need a bit of an

extra boost too if I were taking care of three babies at once."

"Plus their families aren't from here; they moved to Enchanted Enclave for her job. She's only been in town for about ten years. So she and Kyle are on their own in terms of help from extended family. It can't be easy for them."

"I think I remember her now, she's been in once or twice since I started working here, I had no idea she was in that situation."

"Yup. It might be a bit easier for her now that the kids are in school. I think they're all in first grade now."

I shook my head. The whole situation was just so sad. I couldn't imagine what Karen's husband and kids must have been going through.

$\mathcal{I}$ did my best to ignore the rumor mill for the rest of the day. At one point Aunt Lucy came by the coffee shop along with the rest of Lucy's Floozies, as they were known. They were basically a group of Mean Girls – without the meanness – in their fifties and sixties who went around town doing whatever they wished, whenever they wished to do it. They had taken on the name 'Floozies' as their way of reclaiming the word.

"I heard the two of you are the ones who found Karen," Aunt Lucy said as she made her way to the counter while the others, including Leanne's mother, staked out a spot at the biggest table in the place.

"We were," I confirmed.

"There's a rumor going around that Karen died this morning, but don't believe it. I'm pretty sure Ariadne started it. She's been going around accusing Leanne of murder. But Dorothy spoke to Joe just a few minutes ago, and he said Karen's recovering from surgery, but is still very much alive and kicking. Well, ok, she's not kicking since she's unconscious. But she's alive."

"Good," I said, a wave of relief washing over me. Dorothy's husband Joe worked as a police officer here in Enchanted Enclave, so I knew his information would be good. "Ariadne was in here earlier, she told us she thought Leanne should have been arrested for what she did."

"Oh, please," Aunt Lucy said, waving a hand in disgust. "From the way Dorothy said it, you're in the clear, Leanne. With Eliza backing up the story that Karen jumped in front of the car, there's nothing you could have done. Besides, the doctors said the injuries from the accident were superficial at best, and that the only actual issues stem from the fact that someone stabbed her beforehand."

"That's a huge relief," Leanne said. "I was thinking we should convince Kaillie to make some food and send it over for Kyle. He must have his hands full right now with Karen being in the hospital."

"That's a good idea," Aunt Lucy replied. "I imagine he's in Seattle right now. Hopefully he's got someone to take care of the kids, give him a bit of respite. I'm going to talk to the others about this, too. Maybe we can work something out so we can take care of the kids and give him some alone time with Karen while she recovers."

"That would be really good of you, I bet he would be very appreciative," I said. "Especially if the two of them don't have much family support around here. Although, you know, we probably should consider the fact that it's possible he stabbed her."

Leanne looked at me like I was crazy, but Aunt Lucy nodded sagely.

"Yes, that is a consideration. After all, statistically it's most likely that he did it."

"Aunt Lucy!" Leanne said, obviously shocked. "Kyle and Karen always looked like the happiest couple."

"Yes, but you never know what's going on in someone's private life. Never assume that just because someone puts on a happy face on the outside that you know what's going on behind closed doors."

"I guess," Leanne replied. "Still, I can't imagine him being a killer."

"Does Karen live near where we found her?" I asked.

"Not really," Leanne answered. She frowned. "Actually, the thing is, there's not really any houses around there. It's just an empty street. I don't know why Karen would have been there, or who would have stabbed her there. The whole thing is weird."

A sobering thought hit me. "Aunt Lucy... if Kyle really did stab Karen, who's to say that he might not try something else when she's at the hospital?"

"Nothing," Aunt Lucy replied. "Except for the fact that he'd be about a thousand times more likely to get caught. Not only would there be far more people around than on Enchanted Enclave in the middle of the night, but the number of people who know Karen drops down to the single digits down there."

"Right," I said, nodding. "Whereas here on the island it could be one of any number of people."

"Any number of people who would have wanted Karen dead," Leanne mused. "What if she recovers and she has to come back to living here, knowing her murderer is somewhere nearby? It's not like Chief Jones has a great reputation as a crime solver."

I bit my lip. That was a good point. A couple of months ago when I had been accused of murder he had been next to useless.

"Well, we'll see what happens. Anyway, I just wanted to give you the update. Can we have our normal orders?"

"Sure. I'll bring them over in a minute," Leanne said as Aunt Lucy scuttled off to join the rest of the Floozies.

"I guess when your brother and sister are the owners you don't need to pay," I said with a laugh.

"Aunt Lucy once told Aunt Debbie that her payment is her constant presence in her home. I couldn't quite make out what Aunt Debbie muttered in reply but it was something about not being paid enough to deal with Aunt Lucy."

"Yeah, that sounds about right."

Leanne turned to look at me, and spoke suddenly,

like she had wanted to say this for a while but hadn't dared.

"I think I need to find out who stabbed Karen."

"What?" was the only thing I could reply. Had I seriously heard Leanne correctly?

"I'm serious. Chief Ron isn't going to do anything about it. And I hit her with my car. I know everyone except Ariadne is telling me not to feel guilty about it, but I do. I feel so guilty, Eliza. If only I'd paid more attention, if only I'd pressed the brakes a second sooner, or swerved harder, I might not have hit her. I probably still would have stopped to see what was going on, so it's not like it would have changed anything. If she comes out of this – when she comes out of this – I don't want her to have to go around town wondering if the person who killed her is lurking around the corner."

"But Leanne... what if she wakes up and just tells Chief Ron who did this to her? Then that person will be arrested and it'll all be fine."

"I know. And believe me, no one would be happier than me to see that happen. But what if she doesn't wake up? Or what if she doesn't remember? Look, I know you think this is a bad idea, and I'm not asking you to help, but I need to do it."

"Are you joking? Of course I'm going to help you. You not only helped me when I did the same thing, you ended up saving my life. Do you honestly think I'm going to let you do the same without me?"

Growing up, Dad and I had always had each other. We were family, and one thing Dad made sure to instill in me was that when your family needed help, you had to be there. Dad had always been there for me. Leanne had been there for me, even though she barely knew me when I was almost killed trying to solve a murder. And now, it was my turn to repay the favor. In no universe was I going to let her do this alone.

"Oh, you're the best, Eliza," Leanne said, stepping forward and taking me into a big bear hug. "We're going to find out who did this. We just have to."

"Alright, so tell me what you know about Kyle," I said.

"Not a ton, really. He doesn't come in that often. Maybe once a month, so I know him by sight, but that's about it. He works construction here in town."

"Why did Karen and Kyle move here if they don't have any family ties to this place?"

"For the weather. Karen is from Portland, but Kyle's family is on the east coast. They met over there while Karen was in college, got married, but after a few years Kyle decided he had enough of trying to work construction in the middle of winter in Vermont, so they decided to come back out this way. Karen applied to a bunch of jobs, got one here, and so they ended up on Enchanted Enclave. But I think Aunt Lucy is wrong. I don't think Kyle would have done this to her. From everything Karen's said to me about him, and the few times I've seen them together, he seems like a really good guy. He seems to care a lot about Karen."

"Alright, so we're going to have to look into the rest of her life," I said. "What do you know about it?"

Leanne shrugged. "Only that she works at the school. She teaches kids. She seems to enjoy her job, and while she seems quite a bit frazzled when she comes in I figure that's sort of par for the course for a woman trying to juggle a full-time job and triplets."

"What about the other teachers? We should see if we can interview them, find out if someone had something against her. Friends, too."

"Good thinking," Leanne said, snapping her fingers. "I know she's actually good friends with Jack."

Jack Frost was a retired math teacher who had taught both my cousins when they were in high school, and was due in for his morning coffee soon. I hoped he would show up today.

Sure enough, about half an hour later he walked through the door, his normally-friendly face looking a little bit more subdued.

"Good morning, Jack," I greeted him. "I'm sorry about Karen. I heard she's a friend of yours."

"She is, yes," Jack replied. "I couldn't believe it when I heard what happened this morning. Such a huge shame. Who would do something like this to her?" He shook his head sadly before taking out his wallet. I rang through his regular order on the till.

"Do you have any idea who might have done this?" I

asked. "Was there anyone at the school she wasn't getting along with?"

"Well, she had a few disagreements with the principal, lately," Jack said, handing over a ten. "Apparently, the two of them disagreed with how they should handle students who weren't keeping up to standards. Karen wanted to let the parents know, bring them into the loop, and come up with strategies to get the students having a hard time get back up to speed. After all, in Karen's mind, if they fell behind this early in their education, they were never going to catch back up, and it was just going to snowball. Whereas if she could get them back on track now, they'd have better odds of success when they got to high school. Which was a strategy I completely agreed with."

"What did the principal think?"

"He believed that Karen should simply fudge reality a little bit on the report cards, move the child up to the next grade, and let the high school handle it when they got there. Of course, Karen strongly disagreed, and I know they'd had a few meetings about it."

Leanne gave me a hard look. "The school is actually not far from where we found Karen. It's about half a mile away."

"I heard it was you who found her," Jack said. "Thank you. I've been told you're the reason she didn't bleed to death. I appreciate you saving her life. You must be wrong about the principal though. I can't see

Gary Vanderchuck murdering Karen over a simple disagreement."

"What about anyone else at the school? Were there any teachers she disagreed with, or anyone she might have been close to?" I asked.

"You're not thinking of investigating this, are you?"

"No, of course not," Leanne lied smoothly. "We're simply curious. After all, we're the ones who found her; we know what kind of shape she was in. I really hope Chief Jones manages to get the person who did this off the street."

"So do I," I Jack said grimly. "I really cannot think of a nicer person than Karen. And with those kids. Such a tragedy. I can't imagine what Kyle and the boys are going through right now. I don't know who else could have done it. Sasha was her best friend at the school. She could be worth talking to if you really want an idea as to who could have done it."

He took his coffee and chocolate chip banana muffin and left, with Leanne immediately turning towards me.

"I think Gary Vanderchuck should be one of our best suspects. But we need to find Sasha," I said.

"I know her," Leanne said. "She works part-time at the school, mainly as a substitute, but she spends her weekends and days when she's not teaching volunteering at the animal shelter. She'll be there when we close up, we can go and see her then."

That sounded like a good plan.

CHAPTER 5

The rest of the day flew by pretty quickly, but by the time we closed, I was definitely starting to drag.

"Hey Leanne, can you show me how to make a coffee before we go?" I asked.

"Sure," Leanne answered. "It's probably about time you learned how to use the espresso machine, anyway. What do you know about coffee?"

"I know that if there was a way to hook myself up to an IV and inject it directly into my veins, I would do that."

"Alright," Leanne said with a laugh. "So we'll start with the basics. Coffee beans come to the factory raw. You can recognize the raw beans by their color; they're green when they get here. In the back, Dad is in charge of roasting the beans we use here and that we distribute to other coffee shops and stores around the state. Basically, the longer the beans are roasted, the darker they are, and the stronger the flavor. We use our classic medium-roast blend here in the coffee shop."

"Classic Cauldron Blend," I said, nodding. "I've seen the name on the bags when you dump them into the grinder."

"That's the one," Leanne said. "It's got a rich, deep flavor profile, but it's not overly strong. Now, once you have the beans, they need to be ground. That's what this machine here is for." She tapped the top of a large, black machine with a clear funnel at the top that was filled with beans. "I call him Henry. Henry grinds the beans, and gets them ready for use in the machine."

She motioned for me to come closer, and picked up one of the things she used to make the coffee. It was like a metal cup with a long, straight handle coming out of the side.

"This is called the portafilter. Always clean it out with hot water before you start making a new cup of coffee; any old grinds in it have already been used and will simply burn if you run water through them again. I've already cleaned this one for you, so you're going to put the ground up beans into there. Go ahead, try it." She handed me the portafilter and I looked at the grinder. I placed the portafilter underneath it, and then pulled on a lever at the bottom of the grinder, like I'd seen Leanne do.

A small pile of ground coffee fell out of the grinder and right into the portafilter's basket.

"Perfect," Leanne said. "Pull it a second time. I have the grinder set up so that two pulls will give you the exact amount of ground coffee that you need."

I did as she said, and Leanne grabbed a small piece of metal off the counter. It was thicker at the bottom, and designed to fit perfectly in the basket.

"Good. Now, this is a tamper. You're going to press down on the coffee grinds with about thirty pounds of pressure. When we get home you can use the scale to see what thirty pounds is, but I always think of it as a decent, but not excessive amount of pressing. You're going to put some effort in, but it shouldn't be hard."

She handed me the silver tamper and I pressed down on the beans, trying to imagine what thirty pounds of pressure would feel like. When I was done, I looked up, and Leanne nodded approvingly.

"Good. The most important thing once you get the hang of it is to be consistent. If you don't use enough pressure, the coffee will be watery and bland. If you use too much, the water will pass through the beans too slowly and will burn them, giving your coffee a bitter taste. So nail down the pressure, and be consistent."

"Got it. Do it perfectly every time or you'll ruin everything."

Leanne laughed. "Ok, that's a little extreme. There is some leeway. But the sooner you get it down pat, the better. Now that you've got the tampered coffee, you just need to slot it into the machine and press the button with two little cups on it."

"Alright," I said, nodding. I'd seen Leanne do this a hundred times a day for the last six weeks or so, so I was fairly confident I could get it done. I lined up the protruding parts of the portafilter basket with the holes in the coffee machine, slotted it in, and twisted. The portafilter was in solidly, and I pressed the button, grabbing a take-out cup and slotting it under the portafilter.

A couple of seconds later, golden rich crema began to pour from the two nozzles at the bottom of the portafilter and into the cup, like the nectar of the gods. The sweet aroma of roasted coffee floated up to my nostrils and I breathed in deep, inhaling the scent as I closed my eyes. This was perfection.

"That looks pretty good," Leanne said. "Obviously, I'm the best teacher in the world."

"I have to say so," I replied with a grin. "What about the milk?"

"Yeah, so to steam the milk, you want to get the temperature to one hundred and sixty degrees. Again, consistency is key. People come here every day because they know the coffee is going to be good, and they know exactly what they're going to get. Some places just do it by touch, but we use a thermometer, just because they are going to give you the most accurate temperature every single time. Turn off the steamer when you hit a hundred and fifty five degrees; the temperature will climb another five degrees on its own. Fill the jug up to the halfway mark with milk."

I did as Leanne told me. "Alright, so I just put the wand from the steamer into the milk?"

"Give the wand a quick burst of air first, just to get rid of any water that might be in the wand, so it doesn't end up in the milk," Leanne said. "And then yes. You want to steam and stretch the milk. So put the wand in the milk, turn on the steamer, and then lower the milk slowly until you hear a kind of 'kissing' sound."

"That's it, that's the sound," Leanne said a minute later, after I'd followed her instructions. Sure enough there was a slight sound of air being sucked in, and as soon as the thermometer hit one fifty five I turned off the steamer. The temperature gauge rose just a tiny bit further, and I poured the milk into my cup, tilting it slightly.

"Perfect," Leanne smiled. "There you go, you've made your first cup of coffee."

I grinned, grabbed a lid and a sleeve for the cup, and took a sip. The rich, creamy coffee was like silk on my tongue, and I couldn't help but feel accomplished for having made this.

"Do you like it?" Leanne asked.

"I do," I said. "It's delicious."

"Good," Leanne replied. "Tomorrow I'll teach you the differences between the different types of coffee, and then you can try serving customers if you'd like."

"I would like that," I said.

"Anyway, since we're discussing you expanding your work here, what are your long-term plans in life?" Leanne said. "If that's not too personal a question, anyway."

"No, no, that's fine," I replied. "Honestly, I don't know."

"There's always the possibility of going into the family business," Leanne said. "I mean, you might not want to be a barista your whole life, but eventually Aunt Debbie and Dad are going to retire, and I know they won't put any pressure on us, but they're hoping at least one of the cousins has some sort of interest in running the place."

"Are you and Kaillie going to do that?" I asked.

"I would like to. Bossing people around is one of my favorite things to do, so management sounds like a good fit for me," Leanne replied with a wink. "But seriously, I do like the idea of running the whole show. I think I'd be better on Dad's side of things, dealing with distribution, sales, and the more administrative stuff. Kaillie is really happy where she is. She likes being in the kitchen, trying out new recipes, and doing the baking for the day. But there's seriously no pressure, if you decide you want to be like, I don't know, a whale watching tour operator then that's fine too."

I laughed. "I'm not sure that's the thing for me either. To be honest, I don't really know what I want to do. I studied English Literature in college, but that was basically just because I enjoyed it and I didn't know what else to take. I guess I haven't really found my calling in life yet."

"Well, this is a good place to work on that," Leanne said kindly. "You've always got a job here, so you can figure out what it is you want from your life. Plus, the more you chat with the customers and get involved with everything, the more you might find what it is you want to do. That was how I found out I wanted to manage the warehouse side of things. It was by being around everyone and everything."

"And if I decide that my calling in life is to manage the warehouse also?" I asked with a grin.

"Then I will cut you," Leanne threatened, then laughed. "Obviously, I'm kidding. But I do call dibs on that job. You could manage the coffee shop side of things if you wanted, though."

"Fair enough," I said, laughing. "But yeah, I have to admit, I'm not sure what I want to do. Dad was the one who suggested I do my degree. He also thought I should take as many electives as I could in different fields of study, in case one of them tickled my fancy, but none of them really blew me away."

"Oh well, you have lots of time to figure it out," Leanne said. "Anyway, for now, we do have a purpose: we have to go see Sasha at the animal shelter and find out who stabbed Karen."

Kaillie came out from the kitchen just then, with a small tub full of the delicious cookies she'd made earlier under her arm. "Ready to head home?" she asked.

"Actually, Eliza and I were going to go do, uh, something in town first," Leanne said.

Kaillie's eyes narrowed. "Something in town, you say?"

"Yeah. Yoga."

I was fairly certain at least four muscles began to spasm in pain just at the idea of going back to that studio right now.

"You don't have yoga today. You have yoga on Monday, Wednesday and Friday. It's Saturday, remember? And it doesn't start until six. You're going to try and find the person who stabbed Karen, aren't you?"

"What? Why is that the first thing you'd think of? Do you really think so little of me?"

"Yes," Kaillie replied. "It fits your personality perfectly. You're obviously lying about what you're doing, so it's something I would disapprove of. This is Enchanted Enclave, there are only so many ways you can get in trouble, and seeing as Karen was stabbed last night, and looking into that is absolutely the sort of thing you would do, yes, it was my first guess. And given your reaction, that's exactly what you're doing, isn't it?"

"Fine," Leanne replied. "It is. Someone stabbed her, and I want to know who it is."

Kaillie sighed. "You never want me to be able to prove to the paranormal world that our family is deserving of being let back in. Why can't you just be normal?"

"I'm not even a witch; what I do can't factor in," Leanne argued.

"We can't know what factors in. Besides, you're still a part of this family. Your father is a wizard, and you'd be a witch if men could pass down the witch gene. As far as we know, when it comes to evaluating our family and how they're acting, you are considered."

"Well, in that case, they should look favorably on the fact that Eliza and I are putting our lives on the line to find an attempted murderer," Leanne replied.

"Or they're going to look unfavorably on the fact that you're throwing yourself into police investigations when you have absolutely no jurisdiction."

"That's a risk I'm willing to take. We're not going to give up because you're afraid it's going to look bad to some witches and wizards we don't even know."

Kaillie sighed. "I can't believe this. Fine. If you're going to insist on doing this, then I'm going to insist on helping, if only to keep you out of trouble. Where are we going?"

"To the animal shelter. We need to talk to Sasha," Leanne replied without skipping a beat. "Jack Frost told us today that she was good friends with Karen, and we're hoping that she'll be able to tell us about any problems Karen was having, or who might have wanted her dead. We can catch you up on the way; we already have one suspect. We'll need to organize a chat with him, too."

Kaillie sighed. "Why can't you ever do anything without jumping in with both feet and your eyes closed?"

A part of me kind of agreed with Kaillie. Life here on Enchanted Enclave was definitely a roller coaster.

CHAPTER 6

The Enchanted Enclave Animal Shelter was fairly deep in the woods, down a narrow gravel lane, not far from Roman and Leonard Steele's property. The wooden sign at the front was well-worn, but had obviously been painted with care, and the shelter itself was a small but modern building, surrounded by high fences.

As soon as the car pulled up, at least five or six dogs all ran up to the fence, tails wagging and tongues lolling. The space behind the fence was perfect for a bunch of dogs to play in – lots of grass, some trees, toys spread around – the people at the animal shelter obviously cared a lot about their charges.

There were a few excited barks as Leanne, Kaillie and I made our way to the short, wooden building. We stepped inside and found ourselves in a lobby, guarded by a calico-colored cat lying on a small bed on top of the counter, staring at us and wiggling her tail.

Truly a ferocious creature.

I stepped over towards the cat and began patting her, earning myself some happy mews in reply. The whole space was clean, open, and had posters all around with information on taking care of dogs and cats. A moment later a woman with black skin and a natural afro came out from the back with a smile. Her eyes were round and friendly, and her makeup absolutely perfect. She was so pretty I wouldn't have been surprised to see her on the cover of a magazine. Still, her manner was casual and friendly, and I found myself taking an instant liking to her.

"Hi there, welcome to the animal shelter. How can I help you today?"

"Hi, Sasha," Leanne said, taking the lead. "We were given your name by Jack Frost. We wanted to talk to you about Karen."

Sasha's eyes narrowed just a tiny bit. "I'm sorry, I'm not talking to any journalists about her, for her and her family's privacy's sake."

"Oh, no, we're not journalists," Leanne said quickly. "I was the one who found her. Well, Eliza and I were together. I knew Karen from the coffee shop – our family owns Cackling Witch Coffee – and we want to know what happened to Karen as badly as you do."

"I didn't realize," Sasha said, her expression softening. "Thank you. I was told the people who found her saved her life."

"Well, we don't want her coming back to town knowing that the person who tried to kill her is still out there, so we thought we'd ask around and see if we could get an idea of who might have wanted to hurt her. Of course, anything we find out will go to the proper authorities. You know what Chief Jones is like, though."

Sasha sighed. "I do. The thought that he might not be quite up to this has crossed my mind. After all, you were the one who solved the murder of Leonard Steele, weren't you?" she asked, looking and me.

"Yes," I replied. "I didn't really know Karen, since I'm new to town, but from everything I've heard she was a wonderful person, and I think we need to do whatever we can to find out who did this."

Sasha looked at us for a second, made a decision, and nodded. "Yes, you're right. I'll tell you what I know in the hopes that you'll be able to bring the person who tried to kill Karen to justice. Have you heard about the disagreement she had with Gary?"

"The principal at the elementary school?" Leanne replied. "Yes. We were told that Karen wanted to do more to help a few struggling students, but that Gary just wanted her to let it slide and let the teachers at the high school deal with it."

"That's right," Sasha said, nodding. "Gary is very results-oriented. He believes that if we simply bump up the grades for weaker students, then he looks like a good principal, despite the fact that the kids aren't actually learning anything, and that long-term it's a huge detriment to their education. If a child can't do addition properly by the third grade, they're never going to succeed when they have to learn algebra in the eighth grade."

"We know about him, and we will be talking to him," Leanne said. "What about any other teachers? Was there anyone else she was having disagreements with?"

Sasha bit her lip as she thought hard. "No, I can't really think of anyone else who had any problems with her. Not at the school, anyway. She was really quite well-respected."

"What about outside of work?" I asked. "How was her home life?"

Sasha shrugged. "I mean, I think they were happy, overall. Kyle and Karen, that is. They seemed to legitimately care for each other, but they did have their issues. With three boys, all six years old now, it wasn't easy for them. Especially since they had no family in the area. I know Karen was trying to convince her parents to move to Enchanted Enclave to give them a little bit of help. She told me she was feeling overwhelmed since going back to work."

"It was all too much for her?" Leanne asked softly, and Sasha nodded.

"Yes. She wanted to move back to part-time work,

but because of the nature of Kyle's construction job there wasn't enough financial security for them to do it. Karen was feeling burnt out. She was teaching eight-year-olds all day, then coming home and having to cook dinner, take care of their children, and put them to bed."

"Kyle wouldn't help?" I asked, and Sasha gave me a sad smile.

"A little bit, sure. But most women I know who work still end up doing the majority of the housework, even after coming home from a day of working themselves. It was a point of contention for Karen – she was always the one who ended up cooking dinner, who bathed the boys, who put them to bed. Please don't tell anyone I told you this. She'd absolutely hate it if anyone found out. Karen always makes a point of trying to look strong, like she has it all together. She thinks it's important for a teacher to display that kind of resilience. She always wants to set a good example for her students. Even when she wakes up, I'm sure she'll be telling everyone she's fine, and that she doesn't understand what all the fuss is about."

"Yeah, I had no idea," Leanne said. "She seemed a little bit flustered when she came into the coffee shop, but a lot of people do before they get their daily caffeine intake. It just goes to show, you never can know exactly what goes on behind the scenes in peoples' lives."

"Exactly," Sasha said, nodding. "Karen is one of the

strongest women I know. I'm not surprised that she beat the odds and survived being stabbed. I hope she pulls through, for those boys' sake. I'm not saying Kyle is a bad father – he isn't – but a lot of the household responsibilities fell on Karen, and she shouldered a lot of burden."

"I think we understand what you mean," Kaillie said softly. "Do you know if there were financial troubles at all?"

"Oh, no. I mean, money was always tight for them, like it is for everyone these days, but they got by. If there were any major problems, I wasn't aware of them. But you know, that does remind me, I think Karen was having issues with someone."

"Oh?" Leanne prompted, and Sasha nodded slowly.

"Yes, that's right. It's probably nothing, but I should mention it anyway. I don't know the details exactly, but I saw Leanne having a heated argument with the head of the rec center here in town. Do you know him? Andrew Lloyd?"

"I do," Leanne said. "He stops by the coffee shop from time to time."

"Good. I don't know what the argument was about, and I didn't want to interrupt because it looked heated. I asked Karen about it the next time I saw her, and she was very evasive."

"That's interesting," Leanne said slowly. "Thank you for the information."

"Anything I can do to help. I do hope you find the person who tried to kill Karen. Where was she?"

"Down Orca Street, about half a mile away from Main Street."

Sasha frowned. "That's strange, there's not much out there, is there?"

"No," Leanne replied. "I think the closest place is her house, but it still would have been a walk to get to Orca Street from there. And there was the school, but it was still half a mile away. It's a conundrum for sure."

"Alright. Please let me know if there's anything else I can do. Feel free to find me here, or at the school."

"Thanks, Sasha," I said to her. "Are you going to go to the city to see her?"

Sasha nodded. "Yes. As soon as I close up shop here I'm taking the ferry across. I've already told the school board not to schedule me next week; I want to spend some time with Karen, and also take care of the kids for Kyle for a little bit. He's going to need some time to himself, I'm sure."

"That's good of you to do," Kaillie said. "I hope she pulls through."

"Me too," Sasha said. "Thank you again for saving her life."

Leanne didn't say anything, but the guilt was written all over her face. She hadn't forgiven herself for hitting Karen.

The three of us said goodbye to Sasha and headed

back out, each of us lost in our own thoughts as we got into the car.

"It's Saturday afternoon, my guess is we're not going to be able to really talk to anyone else tonight," Kaillie said, and I nodded.

"Agreed. We can get our thoughts ordered and come up with a plan of action, but I think we have a few good suspects to look at."

Leanne put the car into drive as the three of us drove off, leaving the sound of excitedly barking dogs behind us.

CHAPTER 7

"*I*n the name of Saturn, I am exhausted, let's go eat at Mom's place tonight," Kaillie said when we reached the house. Aunt Debbie always made more food than was necessary, since there were often unplanned visitors at the house. I had quickly discovered that it was the unofficial family meeting place.

"Sounds good, Aunt Debbie's food is better than yours anyway," Leanne joked in reply.

"Hey, keep that up and you're not getting any more of these cookies," Kaillie replied, tapping the Tupperware.

"I'd like to see you stop me," Leanne replied.

Kaillie pulled out her wand and tapped the lid. "*Saturn, God of time, keep this box sealed from fingers fine.*"

Leanne scowled. "Now *that's* an unfair use of magic. No wonder you're not seeing any invitations to get back to the paranormal world."

"Take back what you said about my cooking and I'll reverse the spell."

"Fine. Kaillie, cousin dearest, you are the best cook I have ever encountered. Eating food cooked by you is better than any experience I've ever had with a man. You make Gordon Ramsay look like a slob who throws spaghetti at the wall and calls it a meal, and you're way hotter than he is."

I laughed at Leanne's fawning words while Kaillie giggled and reversed the spell.

"See, that's the way you should be treating me every day," Kaillie said.

"Only if you hand over the box of cookies," Leanne said, reaching over, grabbing one and shoving it in her mouth.

"You're going to spoil your appetite," Kaillie said to Leanne.

"Wow, you really are turning into your mother," Leanne replied.

"My body has a separate 'dessert tummy' just for cookies," I said as I reached into the box as well, unable to resist.

Kaillie shook her head at us, then grabbed one herself. Cleopawtra strutted into the room, making sure her entrances were always more like appearances. She was a queen in both name and in actions.

"Welcome back, is there food?" she asked. "I can hear you eating."

"It's not for you, it's got chocolate in it," I said

through a big bite of cookie, and Cleo scrunched her nose at me.

"You're not supposed to talk with your mouth full, that's disgusting."

"You lick yourself on my bed at two in the morning. *That's* disgusting."

"That's grooming," Cleo corrected me. "And besides, that's white chocolate. It's not bad for cats."

"Fine," I grumbled, tearing off a small piece of cookie and handing it over to Cleo, who very happily ate it. "But only because we're going to Aunt Debbie's for dinner, so you won't have any table scraps to beg off me tonight."

"Why would you do that to me?" Cleo whined. "Don't you know I'm a growing kitten?"

"Yeah, a growing kitten with her own food bowl that's filled regularly."

"Human food has superpowers that makes you grow stronger, though."

"I'm fairly certain that's not true."

"It is, every cat knows it."

"Well, I guess you won't be a supercat tonight," I replied.

"Sorry to interrupt what's obviously a riveting conversation," Leanne said, "But I think we should sort out our plan for the next couple of days."

"Yeah, good plan," I replied. "We have Gary, Andrew, and Kyle as suspects."

"Right," Kaillie said. "When was it that the two of

you found Karen?" I couldn't help but notice Kaillie pause before she said 'found' – I had a feeling she was about to say 'ran into', but then thought the better of it, and I was glad for it.

"Well, let's see. Yoga class finished at seven, and it took probably eight or nine minutes to convince Eliza to stop crying and get up off the floor."

I stuck my tongue out at Leanne. "You're not the one who was tortured without any warning."

"Saturn above, you are *whiny*," Leanne said. "It was one yoga class."

"And it's been almost twenty-four hours and I still haven't recovered."

"That's a sign you need to exercise more."

"That's a sign Janice needs to be locked up for cruel and unusual punishment." Although deep down, as much as I didn't want to admit it, I knew Leanne was right. I did need to exercise more. The fact that just an hour earlier I had tried to gauge just how much I *really* needed to pee since the idea of sitting down on the toilet filled me with dread was probably proof enough.

"So let's say we left at five past seven. Maybe add an extra couple of minutes to get into the car, drive off, etcetera," I continued. "We had to have found her at what, quarter past?"

"Probably thereabouts," Leanne said, nodding. "It wouldn't have been later than that."

"And how long do you think it had been since she was stabbed?"

Leanne and I looked at each other. "It couldn't have been long," I said finally. "She was losing blood pretty quickly. Do you think five minutes is right?"

"Yeah, I think that's a good estimate."

"Alright," Kaillie said. "So she was probably stabbed around ten past seven. Do you know where she came from?"

"Well, she was on the left hand side of the road from the car," I said. "But apart from that, I don't know."

"No, me neither," Leanne said. "I didn't see her until we were about a hundred feet from her. I don't know what direction she came from, or if she'd been walking along the road."

"What if we follow the blood?" I asked, snapping my fingers. "Surely there would be traces of it on the road. All we have to do is follow it and see where it leads. Maybe that'll tell us where Karen was when she was stabbed."

Kaillie glanced out the window. "We probably have just enough time to go have a look before the sun goes down and it's time to go have dinner."

"It's too bad your familiar isn't a dog; the nose could have come in handy."

"*Excuse me?*" Cleo replied, obviously outraged. "Your friend needs to learn some manners. I am superior to a dog in every respect."

"I know," I whispered to Cleo. "I'm sorry. She doesn't mean anything by it. We're going to go out, but we'll be back soon."

"In time for my dinner to be served, I hope."

"Of course, how could I ever forget?"

Satisfied she wasn't going to starve to death, Cleo curled herself up into a ball and went to sleep while the three of us got ready to go out once more. We were only a half mile from where we had found Karen, so decided that it was easier to walk than to take the car. About five minutes later, we were at the spot.

At least, I figured it was the spot. Leanne was the expert, having lived here her whole life. To me, this place in the day looked completely different. The trees lining the side of the road were far less ominous-looking, for one thing.

"This was it," Leanne said, looking down on the ground. "There. That dark patch there; that had to be where she was when we found her."

I looked to where Leanne pointed, and sure enough, there was a tiny patch of asphalt that looked just a bit darker than the rest.

"Alright, so she came from this direction," I said, moving towards the trees. "Here's another spot. We have to just follow this trail."

While I had initially thought it would be pretty easy to follow the trail, it turned out that wasn't the case at all. There just hadn't been all that much blood that had dripped onto the ground, and even though we were able to find a spot here and there, they weren't all that obvious, and with the sun edging closer and closer to the horizon, the available light was fading fast.

"Can you use a spell to find it?" Leanne asked, and Kaillie bit her lip, looking hesitant. "Come on, it's not like there's anyone around who will see."

"Fine," Kaillie said, looking around carefully to confirm there were no cars or people nearby. *"Saturn, god of wealth, reveal the blood that lays here in stealth."*

I gasped as Kaillie moved her wand around, and tiny specks on the pavement suddenly began glowing blue. We now had a trail to follow. Kaillie held the wand steady while Leanne and I followed the path of blood, which continued for about two hundred feet before suddenly ending in the middle of the road.

"That's weird," Kaillie said with a frown. "There's nothing in the forest nearby?"

"No," I said, making my way to the edge of the woods and looking in. The darkness made the blue glow from the spell obvious; there was definitely no blood in the forest.

"She must have been in a car," Kaillie said, putting her wand away and ending the spell. "She was stabbed in a vehicle, and must have either been pushed out or managed to jump out. Whoever attacked her then sped off."

"That makes perfect sense," Leanne said, nodding. "I think you're right. Look at that, we have a clue!"

It was certainly a start.

CHAPTER 8

The three of us headed back to the house, where I quickly left some food out for a napping Cleopawtra before continuing on further down the street to Aunt Debbie's. The three of us walked right in, and as soon as we did the sound of an argument between Aunt Debbie and Aunt Lucy reached our ears. I raised my eyebrows as my eyes met Leanne's, and she shrugged.

"You know you're not supposed to goad her," I could hear Aunt Debbie saying.

"Who says?" came my other aunt's reply.

"The fact that you're almost sixty years old and you're supposed to be better than that."

"Well, she's nearly the same age as I am and she thinks it's alright to pick on a woman forty years younger than her."

"You're not supposed to argue with an idiot. They'll

drag you down to their level and beat you with experience."

"Oh please. Ariadne might be an idiot, but I have so much experience beating her over the years I can do it in my sleep."

"You're going to end up with another visit from Kyran," Aunt Debbie warned as the three of us stepped into the kitchen. As soon as the two witches noticed us, they immediately dropped the topic of conversation.

"Why hello there," Aunt Debbie said, beaming at us. "Joining us for dinner? We're doing burrito bowls tonight."

"What did Aunt Lucy do to Ariadne?" Leanne asked with a grin, and Aunt Debbie glared at her sister.

"You weren't supposed to hear any of that. And it's none of your business."

"It sounds like it definitely is my business," Leanne said. "After all, I'm the one Ariadne came into the coffee shop basically accusing of murder."

"What you don't know is that this afternoon she went to see Chief Ron and tried to convince him that you deserved to be arrested for what you did. Luckily, he wasn't alone, and that young detective, what's his name, came over and sorted everything out. He not-so-politely told Ariadne she was interfering with affairs that weren't any of her business and escorted her out of the police station."

"Ross Andrews?" I offered up hopefully, and Aunt Lucy nodded.

"That was him. He's a nice young man. Anyway, I found out about this, and let's just say Ariadne's store suddenly found itself to be home to an infestation of frogs that she wasn't expecting."

I stifled a laugh as I imagined the gift shop full of overly-perfumed kitsch being overrun by amphibians, and Ariadne having no idea how to deal with it.

"Aunt Lucy!" Kaillie cried. "You're not supposed to use magic like that, not in front of humans."

Aunt Lucy shrugged. "How will anyone ever know? We live on an island that's full of nature. Frogs are par for the course."

"Well, apart from the fact that Ariadne came and accused you of doing it," Aunt Denise said.

"She thinks I bought the frogs from Tim down on the water. She doesn't think I used magic," Aunt Lucy retorted. "Seriously, I did think this through."

"I, for one, am glad that my aunt was willing to defend my honor," Leanne replied with a grin as Uncle Bob walked into the room as well. "Oh, hey Dad."

"Hey, sweetie," the wizard replied, making his way over to Leanne and kissing her lightly on the forehead while giving her a quick squeeze. "I thought I'd come by and enjoy dinner with my sisters, but it's a nice surprise to have the rest of the family here."

"We had a long day," Kaillie said. "And according to Leanne, Mom's cooking is better than mine anyway."

"I'm not sure that's true anymore," Aunt Debbie said. "Anyway, I hope you all like burrito bowls, even though it'll mean Mexican two days in a row. I was just getting it all ready when Lucy walked in. The dishes are ready to go on the table."

Aunt Debbie muttered a spell under her breath and two of the cupboard doors, along with one of the drawers opened up and an extra three sets of plates, glasses and cutlery flew out and launched towards the dining room, landing on the table in perfect formation.

The six of us made our way into the dining room and sat down. The next few minutes were spent with everyone busying themselves making up their bowls and passing the various ingredients around the room.

When everyone was settled and had taken a few bites conversation began once more.

"Do you have any more updates on Karen's condition?" Leanne asked Aunt Lucy, who nodded.

"Yes. Dorothy heard from Joe that Karen is out of surgery and the cops were able to speak with her for a few minutes. She has no memory of what happened; the last thing she remembers from that day was the end of the school day and her students leaving. After that, nothing."

"So she has no idea who did this to her," I said.

"That's right," Aunt Lucy confirmed. "It's too bad, really. It would have been nice to have the person who did this caught."

"Karen is expected to make a full recovery, then?" Kaillie asked hopefully.

"Yes. She's really lucky, from what I've heard. She

lost a lot of blood. They're going to move her from the hospital in Seattle back to Enchanted Enclave in a few days. She'll need to stay there for a bit longer, just to make sure there are no complications, but she wants to come back home and the doctors think it should be safe for her to make the journey back in a day or two."

"Good," Uncle Bob said. "Although I don't like the idea that the person who did this to her is still walking around."

"It's probably easier for his family if they're back home as well," Aunt Debbie mused. "After all, it's probably nicer for Kyle and the boys if they're able to sleep in their own beds. Plus, there are more people up here willing to help out. And with Karen's family having come up from Portland, they'd probably be happier in Karen's home than in a hotel."

"They're going to have to beef up security at the hospital," Uncle Bob said, and Leanne shrugged.

"They'll do it, but I'm not sure the killer will have a second bite at the apple. Not when Karen's in the hospital, anyway. After all, this is Enchanted Enclave. If we know that Karen has no idea who stabbed her, then the person doesn't have to worry about Karen telling on them. At the very least, they would wait until Karen is away from a building with security cameras all over the place," she replied.

"Maybe," Aunt Lucy said. "I still think it's most likely the husband did it."

"We found out you were right about that, too, Aunt Lucy," Leanne said.

"That's not a surprise at all. But right about what specifically this time?"

I hid a smile as I answered. "There were problems in Kyle and Karen's marriage surrounding the amount of work Karen had to do. She was working full time and then taking care of the kids as soon as she got home, and she resented Kyle for it. She wanted to move to working part-time but they couldn't afford it."

Aunt Lucy snorted. "That's always the way, though. Most men still seem to think that even though women are allowed to work outside the home now they should still be taking care of all the household chores, too. It's one of the reasons I never got married."

"That, and there isn't a man in this world who'd be able to survive living with you for that long," Uncle Bob muttered under his breath, and Aunt Lucy glared at him.

"I heard that," she replied. "I'll have you know I had plenty of suitors back in my day. Saturn knows I still do now, in the prime of my life. Hit it and quit it, that's my motto."

Kaillie choked on the forkful of food in her mouth and was hit by a coughing fit that lasted a solid thirty seconds.

"Lucy," Aunt Debbie scolded. "That's not appropriate."

Aunt Lucy shrugged. "It's true, though. Deny it all

you want, but we both know women still deal with an uneven share of the housework in most families. In a family where that involves taking care of triplets, I'm not surprised that Karen was feeling stressed."

"Still, you would think that would lead to her wanting to kill Kyle, not the other way around," I mused.

Aunt Lucy shrugged. "We don't know what happened, remember? Maybe she came at him first."

It was always possible.

"That wasn't a problem with you though, Dad, was it?" Leanne asked, turning to Uncle Bob.

"It wasn't, no. Your mom and I split up for completely different reasons. Although I do have to admit, early on in the marriage I did fall back into traditional gender roles. I would come back from work, crack open a beer and hang out on the couch like I used to when I was single. Your mom would come home from working at the bank, and I'd let her cook dinner and deal with all the chores like laundry and the dishes. She'd ask me for help, telling me she'd spent the whole day working too, and I'd make some noncommittal noise and go back to the TV."

"So how did she get things to change?" Leanne asked, and Uncle Bob grinned.

"Eventually she also just stopped doing any housework. She'd join me on the couch after work, and left absolutely everything. It took about a week before the house got so disgusting that I yelled at her for not doing it. She replied that if I wasn't going to give her a hand, then she wasn't going to do it either, and that we could either live in filth, get divorced, or I could carry my own weight."

"I'm guessing the third option won out," Leanne replied, and Uncle Bob shrugged.

"If I'd gone for either of the other two options you wouldn't be here, and I've never regretted the choice I made," he replied. "Besides, the thing is, Laura was completely right. I was being selfish, and I was just assuming that because Laura was the wife it was her job to keep a home, even though we were both working full-time. I came to understand that eventually. We were partners. I wasn't "helping her" take care of the home, I was helping take care of the home I lived in. I was just lucky that I had a wife who was willing to call me out on my crap when we were newlyweds instead of one who stewed and let resentment get the better of her. Our marriage probably wouldn't have lasted as long as it did if we'd done that."

"Well, regardless of whether or not it was Kyle who tried to kill her, I think so long as Karen remains in the hospital she's safe," Leanne said. "So the cops will have a few days to try and figure out who killed her."

"Yes, the cops," Aunt Lucy replied, a knowing look in her eyes. I had a sneaking suspicion she was well aware of what the three of us were doing.

Kaillie suddenly became intently focused on taking a huge bite of her burrito bowl while Leanne stared

Aunt Lucy down, as if daring her to reveal what we were doing to the rest of the family.

Luckily, if anyone else noticed the scene, they pretended not to, and the conversation quickly moved on to other topics.

CHAPTER 9

*T*he next morning at the coffee shop was fairly uneventful, with the day always starting a little bit more slowly for everyone on Sundays. Leanne took the opportunity to start teaching me how to make the different types of coffee.

"The most common coffee we make with the machine is a latte," Leanne explained. "That's essentially stretched milk on the bottom, with about a quarter inch of foam on top."

"Ok," I said, as Leanne showed me how to pour the stretched milk from the bottom of the jug first, and then slow down the pour to allow the foam to come out on top.

"If you decide to get artistic with it you can do some pretty cool latte art. Don't tell Kaillie I said this, but I bet you could figure out some spells to make some pretty amazing stuff. Of course, you're probably a few years away from being able to do that. You'd have to come up with the spells yourself, since I don't think the family knows any now."

"Can witches invent spells?" I asked, and Leanne nodded.

"I think so, yeah. If anyone would know about that it's Aunt Lucy, and not me, the one person in the family with no magical powers," she replied bitterly. "I'm pretty sure Aunt Lucy has done it a few times. I've seen her use spells that were so strange I can't imagine they were passed down through the generations."

"That sounds like her," I said with a smile.

"Now, another order we get a decent amount of is a macchiato. You pour those into the espresso cups, and then you add just a little bit of foam to the espresso, about a tablespoon's worth. When you're making a macchiato, you *really* can't mess up the coffee. It's basically an espresso shot with a tiny bit of milk, so if you've burned the beans at all, the customer will be able to taste it."

"What do I do if I've messed it up?" I asked.

"You can always just throw out that shot," Leanne replied. "We're a coffee company, and that's the one thing we do. The most important thing for customers is that they get a good coffee every time. My goal every time I pull a shot is to make sure the customer is getting the best experience they can. If that means throwing out a few here and there because I over-tamped the beans or forgot to clean out the portafilter before making it, then so be it. Aunt Debbie and Dad will never get mad at you for doing that. We'd all rather you err on the side of caution rather than serve someone a bad coffee."

"That's a really good attitude," I said with a smile. "I'm glad to know I'm not expected to get it right every time."

"We all mess up sometimes," Leanne said with a wink as the front door opened and we turned to greet our first customer of the day.

I gasped slightly when I saw him; he was tall, with dark brown hair and eyes like ice. His pointed ears betrayed the fact that he wasn't human: it was Kyran, an elf I had met and the only paranormal I knew outside of our family.

"Hey, Kyran," Leanne greeted him with a smile. "Want a coffee?"

"I might, actually," he said.

"Mind if Eliza makes it? She's just learning, so it'll be free if she does."

Kyran laughed. "Sounds good. I'm sure she'll be fine."

"Thanks," I said quietly as I made my way to the machine. I had to admit, it was a lot more nerve-wracking than I thought it would be to make coffee for someone else, even if they weren't paying for it. Last night, the stakes were low: the only person who was going to suffer if I messed it up really badly was me.

I took a deep breath and mentally went through all the steps Leanne had taught me the night before while she had a chat with Kyran.

"So what brings you to town today?"

"There were reports that someone in this area used magic to generate three hundred frogs yesterday," Kyran replied. "Naturally, I thought of Lucy. Is she around?"

"She's not here," Leanne said. "That doesn't sound like her, though."

"That sounds exactly like her, that's why she was the first person I thought of," Kyran replied, laughing.

"Don't tell Kaillie you found out about it," Leanne warned. "She's so sensitive about Aunt Lucy doing things that prove we still deserve our banishment."

"Fair enough," Kyran replied as I finished making the coffee and placed the to-go cup in front of him.

"Can you let me know if that's alright?" I asked cautiously, and Kyran nodded with a smile.

"Sure." He took a long sip, then nodded and looked at me approvingly. "This is really good. Nice job."

I smile of satisfaction spread across my face. I had done it! I had made coffee for someone else, and it hadn't been completely disgusting.

"How are you settling in with your family?" Kyran continued. "Are you getting used to being able to use magic?"

"A little bit," I said. "It's hard, though. I've been trying some more advanced spells, like changing the weather, which while it's advanced, should be an easy thing for an air coven witch like myself to do, but I just can't do it right. The other day I tried to make the sunny day turn cloudy, and all that happened was a single cloud shaped like Calvin from *Calvin and Hobbes* appeared, and he made it rain, just like on those bumper stickers you see. Aunt Lucy fixed it for me, but not before the whole thing went viral on the internet."

Kyran bit back a smile. "I heard about that, too. I kind of figured it might have been you, although the image also made me think of Aunt Lucy. If you don't mind, I might come by with Tina sometime. She'll be able to help."

"That would be great," I replied gratefully. "I'm sorry I used magic and ended up all over the internet. I swear I didn't mean it."

"I know," Kyran said. "I've reported your situation back to the people I know in the paranormal world, and they're aware that there's going to be a learning curve for you. However, they also think it's important that you embrace your magical powers, and so if it results in a few mishaps that need to be cleaned up here and there, they're alright with that."

I breathed a sigh of relief. I knew Kaillie wasn't mad at me about the whole Calvin cloud situation – she understood that I was trying a more difficult spell than I was used to – but I still felt bad knowing that she was so intent on one day proving our family deserved access to the paranormal world once more, and doing something that garnered so much attention. It was really the number one no-no for witches in the regular human world.

I was going to have to tell Kaillie what Kyran just told me. Hopefully it would put her mind at ease.

"Alright, I'm going to go find your Aunt and tell her it's not subtle when she conjures up a bunch of frogs just because she's mad at Ariadne."

I smiled. "It sounds like this isn't the first time you've had to come pay Aunt Lucy a visit for that exact reason."

"You'd be right there," Kyran replied with a good-natured laugh. "Ah, well. I prefer dealing with your aunt than hunting down vampires who murder humans for the underground blood market."

I gasped. "That's a real thing?"

"Absolutely," Kyran replied. "I do my best to stop it, but I can't be everywhere at once."

"Well, that's not a nice thought," I said.

"Don't worry. It's actually quite rare. A few hundred years ago when I started it was much more common, but the paranormal world has passed some strict laws regarding the use of human blood, and now the vampires know that I'm out looking for them, and that I will come after them. They know it's not worth it anymore, for the most part."

"Good to know," I said.

"Alright, I'll see you when I see you," Kyran said. "Thanks again for the coffee."

He lifted his cup to me as if to toast me, and headed out the door to continue his search for Aunt Lucy.

CHAPTER 10

I wasn't really expecting to see Kyran's girlfriend anytime soon. I mean, what did time even mean to an elf? I was told they were immortal, and Kyran had confirmed himself that he was at least hundreds of years old. For all I knew he might tell her a year from now, and that would feel like a day to him.

That was why I was incredibly surprised when she walked into the coffee shop that afternoon, about an hour before we were set to close.

The coffee shop was practically empty by then, with just a couple of customers sitting at their tables enjoying a late-afternoon caffeine hit before heading home for the evening. A woman with long, brown hair and blue eyes walked into the coffee shop, followed closely by two other women – one with wavy brown hair who looked around at everything like it was the first time she'd ever seen a coffee shop, and another with red hair, green eyes, and more freckles than I'd ever seen on a person.

"Hi," I greeted the three of them, assuming they were tourists. "What can I get for you?"

"I'll have a vanilla latte please," the woman replied. "What do you guys want?"

"How do you order coffee in the human world?" the second one asked.

"I'm guessing you can't add potions to these ones?" the third said. "I'll just have a hot chocolate. It's too late in the day for coffee and I have to train early tomorrow."

"You order it like any other coffee, Ellie," the first woman replied.

"Fine, I'll have a latte, but I also want to try one of these muffins. Has anything been added to them?" the second woman asked, peering closely at one of the two lemon poppyseed muffins we had left.

"Well, they're made with fresh lemon zest," I offered, but Ellie shook her head.

"No, silly. I mean *potions*. Have these muffins been magically enhanced?"

My mouth dropped open, and the first witch smiled. "I'm sorry, we should have introduced ourselves. I'm Tina, Kyran's fiancé. Wow, it feels awesome to say that," she added, a blush rising up her face as she lightly fingered the small, but elegant diamond ring on her finger.

"Aww, congratulations," I gushed, and while the red shade of Tina's face grew deeper, at the same time a smile of pure joy spread across it.

"Thanks. He proposed to me just the other night and I couldn't be happier. This is Ellie, by the way," she said, motioning to the woman who had asked about the muffins. "And Sara."

"Isn't that ring gorgeous?" Ellie said, looking proudly on at her friend. "It's so elegant and strong, just like Tina."

"We all knew it was just a matter of time before he proposed to her," Sara said. "They're just perfect for one another."

"They really are. I'm thinking a summer wedding would be perfect. I'm trying to convince them a destination wedding would be fantastic. Maybe Mexico."

Tina laughed. "Yeah, I'm sure Kyran with his super pale elf skin would just *love* Mexico. Honestly, I don't care where we get married. I just want to spend the rest of my life with Kyran, and I want you guys to be there when we celebrate our love."

"Stop it, you're going to make me cry," Sara complained.

"Alright, moving on, no one answered my question about the potion."

"There's no magic in any of the baked goods. My cousin Kaillie has a hang-up about using them in food being served to people," Leanne said. "She's the one who does all the baking."

"Wow, if I were a witch in a world full of humans I'd be using magic in *everything*," Ellie said, looking closely at the food. "Can I try one of them anyway?"

"Sure," I said, grabbing one of the muffins for her and putting it in the microwave for a few seconds.

"Kaillie doesn't like the fact that we've been banished from the paranormal world and is super conscious about doing anything that might make us seem like bad witches. She considers giving potions to people to be one of those things. Personally, I wouldn't mind, and I love taking potions that help make life easier, but I guess I'm in a rather unique situation," Leanne continued.

"So you must be Leanne, then," Tina said with a smile. "Kyran told me about you. Your father is a wizard, so you know all about magic, but you have no powers of your own."

"Yeah, and it sucks. You have no idea how much I could use magic. I'd be using it all the time. Magic is wasted on Kaillie; of the two cousins I should have been the one to get the powers. She won't even use them to give her baked goods a bit of a boost."

"I have to say, these are very good," Ellie said, taking a bite of the muffin I handed her a moment earlier. "Where is Kaillie? I'm going to see if I can't get that recipe off her; I think these would do really well at The Witching Flour. I can see it now: Feel Powerful Poppy seed and Lemon muffins. Great for that morning when you're going in asking your boss for a raise." Ellie lifted her arms and moved them across like there was an invisible banner announcing the muffins.

"Kaillie is just at the back," Leanne said, motioning towards the door leading to the kitchen. "Feel free to head over there and have a chat with her."

"And try to get her new recipe for raspberry and white chocolate cookies, too," I said. "They're absolutely divine."

"Will do, thanks for the tip," Ellie said with a grin as she made her way towards the door leading to the kitchen. Leanne motioned to Sara and the two of them left the counter area.

"So you're Eliza," Tina said to me, and I nodded.

"That's right. I'm the one who grew up here and had no idea I was a witch until about a month ago. It's been quite the discovery, let me tell you."

Tina laughed good-naturedly. "You don't have to. I've actually been through your exact same situation. Almost two years ago, I fell through a tree in downtown Seattle that was actually a portal to the paranormal world. That was how I found out I was a witch."

"What about your parents? Didn't they know?"

Tina gave me a small smile. "My mother died, and my father... well, it's complicated. I was abandoned in Seattle and adopted by a wonderful couple that I consider to be my parents. They passed away before I found out I was a witch."

"Oh, I'm sorry. My mom died when I was a baby, and my father only recently. It's so heart-wrenching."

"It really is," Tina agreed. "How have you been finding your introduction to magic? Kyran tells me you've been having some trouble with more advanced spells?"

I nodded. "Yes. It's been a lot of fun, I have to say. I am enjoying the lessons, but it's hard to try and cast spells when you're around humans and you have to hide the fact that you can do magic. And I don't quite know what to do when I get a spell wrong. How do I reverse something that's incorrect in the first place? How can I try to catch up to everyone else fast enough? Kaillie has twenty-plus years of spell casting experience on me. I don't know. I guess I just feel a little bit overwhelmed, and I'm afraid of... I guess of messing everything up somehow. I'm worried that I'm going to make a big mistake, or multiple big mistakes, which I have to be especially cautious about given how there are people all over the place who can't know about magic."

I was expecting Tina to tell me I was just being silly, but to my surprise, she nodded in reply. "I know just how you feel. I went through a lot of those same feelings myself. Of course, I didn't have to deal with the added pressure of not being able to use magic in front of humans, so it must be even worse for you that way. How has your family been? Are they supportive?"

"They're wonderful, actually," I said. "So much more

so than I could have expected. Dad never wanted me to know them, and I guess he had his reasons - apparently, he never quite liked the fact that Mom was a witch - but they've been nothing but supportive and friendly. Everyone has done whatever they can to make me feel at home."

"That's good," Tina said. "And I'm guessing you're a little bit hesitant to let them know about everything you're feeling?"

I nodded. "Yeah, if I'm completely honest, I think I am. I just feel… inadequate. Everyone else knows what they're doing, and I don't. Plus, I'm just getting used to trusting other people. It had always been Dad and me. And it's really cool that I have this new family and all, and I love them, but I'm not the type to bare my heart open without building up a significant amount of trust first." It was funny; I didn't know Tina at all, but she was easy to talk to. Maybe it was the fact that she lived in a completely different world. Or maybe it was because she had been through exactly the same thing I did. It might have also been the way she didn't seem to judge me at all, but something about Tina made me want to tell her everything.

"If I can give you one piece of advice, it would be to let go of that hesitation and try to take the leap and ask for what you need," Tina said. "Having a supportive group of friends or family is the most important thing in the world. You need that support network, and it sounds like you have it, so use it. They'll be happy to help you. They *want* to help you, and if you let them in, trust me, the results can be spectacular."

"Thanks," I said with a small smile. "I appreciate it."

"Another thing that's so important when you're casting spells is confidence. If you're not one hundred percent dedicated to the spell, it just won't work. It takes time to build that kind of confidence, and it's easier to build it with simpler spells. You might want to try absolutely nailing them before you move on to the others, even though I know it's tempting. And try to focus on spells that you can do inside your home, with the blinds drawn. It'll probably be easier for you to feel completely confident when you're working magic with no chance of any humans being able to see you."

"That's great advice," I said. "I wish I'd thought of it. I think the others mean well, but they can't understand what it's like to come into these powers so late in life."

"You're right, they can't. You're going to have to help them understand it. They probably don't think about things like being worried about casting spells in front of humans because they've been avoiding doing it their whole lives. But if you let them know, I'm sure they'll try harder for you. As for how to reverse spells – make sure someone else who can do magic is around when you're casting spells to start with. That way, you can give it a shot, and if you mess it up, someone else can fix it before it becomes a problem. Of course, sometimes spells go wrong and they end up being a good thing. Sara trying to stop me from falling off my broom and completely messing up the spell is how we got a swimming pool in the backyard," Tina said with a laugh.

"That sounds like a story I'd love to hear over all the drinks I'm going to buy you for this amazing advice," I said. "That is, if you're willing to stay for a little while longer."

"That's very sweet of you. I'll ask the others, but I'm sure they'll be happy. I assume Ellie has found someone who likes baking as much as she does, and Leanne seems happy to explain the concept of radiators to Sara," she said, and I looked over to where Leanne was pointing at the pipe at the bottom of the radiator in the corner while Sara put her hands up close to it to feel the heat.

I laughed. "I guess they're not a thing in the paranormal world?"

"Nope, basically all heating is done by magic."

"That's insane. I can't imagine. I thought finding out I was a witch and moving north two states was about as crazy as things could get."

"You have no idea," Tina said with a laugh, then quickly covered her mouth as if realizing what she had said. "Sorry. I don't want to make you feel bad about the fact that you can't go there."

"Don't worry about it," I said, shaking my head. "Kaillie would love to travel to the paranormal world more than anything, but frankly, right now, I think this has been enough of a life change on its own. I'm not sure I could handle an entire new world on top of that, and I'm in awe of you for managing to not only discover you were a witch, but also get used to being one in a whole magical land."

Tina smiled. "Thanks. It wasn't easy, I will say that."

"What are your plans for the rest of the afternoon?" I asked.

"We're pretty open. We didn't know what you'd want to do, if you wanted to practice some magic with us, if you wanted to just chat somewhere, if you wanted us to go away and leave you alone. We're fine with whatever. Amy, one of our other friends, is back in Western Woods holding down the fort, which basically means making sure the familiars don't burn the house down if we're not back in time for dinner."

I laughed. "Boy does that sound, well, familiar. Mine is a cat named Cleopawtra, and boy oh boy does she ever live up to her queenly name."

"Mine is a cat named Mr. Meowgi who thinks he's a martial arts expert. Which reminds me, I would like to stop somewhere that sells DVDs and pick up a few things for him to watch."

"Sure, Kaillie and Leanne will know where to go for that."

The conversation moved on, and before I knew it, the two customers in the shop had left, and closing time had come and gone. Aunt Debbie came out from her office and looked at us in surprise. "Haven't the two of you started cleaning up yet?" she asked Leanne and me.

Whoops. We had gotten so caught up in getting to know the witches from Western Woods that I'd completely forgotten about closing up.

"Hey, Aunt Debbie, these are witches from the paranormal world," Leanne said. "Kyran asked them to come by, since Tina only found out she was a witch a couple years ago."

"Oh, how lovely," Aunt Debbie said, looking approvingly at Tina and the others. "What coven do you belong to?"

"Jupiter," Tina answered proudly. "We're from the coven of Jupiter."

"Ah, a lightning coven," Aunt Debbie said. "Good for you. Well, I'm sure you don't want to spend your time speaking with an oldie like me. Leanne, if you all want to leave and spend some extra time getting to know each other, I can handle closing here."

"Thanks, Aunt Debbie," Leanne said. "That would be awesome. Let me just go grab Kaillie and Ellie and tell them we're ready to go."

CHAPTER 11

*F*ifteen minutes later the six of us were piled into a booth at Otterly Delicious, having placed our orders.

"I haven't been to the human world since we came with Tina to grab her stuff when she first moved to the paranormal world," Ellie said, looking around. "It's so quaint. Look at the skills that human has, balancing that huge tray of food instead of just using a wand to move it around."

"You probably shouldn't be calling them 'humans' out here so loudly," Sara warned. "People will think you're a psychopath. They're called 'people', right?"

"That's right," I said, doing my best to hide my amusement.

"So apart from teaching Eliza here how to be a witch, what do you guys do out here?" Sara asked.

"Well, right now we're trying to solve an attempted

murder," Leanne replied. "Although I'm not sure that falls under the category of normal fun things we do."

To my surprise, Ellie clapped her hands together. "Oh good, let us help! It's been ages since we've gotten to help solve a good murder."

"Seriously?" Kaillie asked, her mouth dropping open.

"We're not Enforcers or anything like that. We're not even private investigators," Tina said quickly. "But after I arrived in Western Woods there were a string of crimes committed, and for various reasons we ended up thinking we were the best people to solve them."

"We were right basically every time, too," Ellie said, crossing her arms.

"Yeah, when we didn't almost die," Sara replied.

"Oh please. We never did die, and that's just the cost of justice," Ellie said, waving away Sara's concerns. "Anyway, spill. Who almost got murdered, and what have you got so far?"

Leanne immediately began telling the whole story, giving the Western Woods witches the entire low-down on what had happened, what we knew, and who we suspected. As soon as she finished, the waitress arrived with our food, and we spent a few minutes digging in while the other witches digested the information.

I'd ordered the chicken carbonara, and the creamy pasta did not disappoint.

"So," Ellie said when we'd all enjoyed a few bites

and taken the edge off our hunger. "You've got three suspects. I assume Kyle is still in Seattle with Karen?"

"Yeah, as far as I know," I replied. "And to be honest, I think we should probably do as much as we can without having to talk to him. Life is probably pretty traumatic for him right now if he's not the murderer."

"That's a good point," Sara said. "Although personally, I really like him for the murder."

"You do?" Kaillie asked. Sara nodded.

"Yeah. We have some of the same problems in the paranormal world, where witches are expected to do a lot more of the work. Of course, it's slightly different. Dishes and the like can be cleaned with a wave of the wand. But little witchlings and wizardlings still need to be taken care of, and that often falls on the witch, even when she also has a job."

"You and Kyran are going to have to figure out how that's going to work out with the two of you," Ellie said to Tina, giving her a light nudge in the ribs. "After all, Kyran is what, hundreds of years old? Maybe thousands? He's probably pretty set in his ways."

"Please," Tina scoffed. "Have you seen his place? Kyran is neater than I am. Besides, you know he's not a typical elf. We'll be fine."

"I know, I'm just teasing you," Ellie said. "The two of you are going to live a fantastic life together. Although I am going to miss having you around the house."

"Hey, it's not like I'm going to be far," Tina said. "I'll still come and visit. Besides, with all of my studies to become an Animal Healer, I'm going to need a lot of help from Amy. And I'll still help out at The Witching Flour when you need a hand."

"Good," Ellie said. "Now, about solving this murder. Six heads are better than three, and frankly, I miss these sorts of things. Besides, this is just a human world murder. How hard could it be to solve?"

"Truly spoken like a witch who has never spent much time here," Tina said, smiling. "But I agree; while we're here, we might as well help."

"It's a good thing Amy didn't come after all," Sara said with a laugh. "She'd love to tell us all about how this is a terrible idea, and that butting our noses into things in Western Woods was bad enough, but doing it in the human world is worse."

"She sounds like she'd get along really well with Kaillie," Leanne joked, earning herself a scowl from her cousin.

"Why don't the two of us go and check out Karen's place?" I suggested to Tina. "We can continue our chat while committing felonies."

"My favorite late Sunday activity," she replied with a wink.

"Good plan," Leanne said. "I'll take Sara and we can go speak with Gary Vanderchuck. He's at the gym every Sunday night, so we'll be able to "accidentally" run into him there."

"That leaves Kaillie and me to go see Andrew," Ellie said.

"That works for me. Only one rule though: no magic."

"Well that's no fun," Ellie replied.

"You're not the one whose family was banished from the paranormal world. I don't want to do anything that could get us more on the bad side of those in charge than we already are."

"Fine," Ellie finally conceded. "We won't use any magic. It'll be like an adventure, pretending to be a human investigator for a day."

I laughed at the excitement Ellie seemed to feel about it. What must it have been like growing up in the paranormal world, where not using magic was some sort of strange exotic life she couldn't even imagine?

"Hey, some of us don't have any choice," Leanne said.

"We'll meet back at the house when we're all done," Kaillie added. "We can compare notes and maybe we'll have a better idea as to who the killer might be."

"Sounds good," I replied with a nod. "Let's do it."

The six of us finished off our meals, then headed off in pairs to investigate the murder.

"So where is Karen's house?" Tina asked.

"I got the address off Ellie earlier, it's down this way," I said. "It should only be a ten minute walk, if you don't mind."

"Sure. I got really used to walking around Western Woods, since I'm not the most comfortable witch on a broom, and there are no cars there."

"I feel you there," I replied. "I actually found out I was a witch when I grabbed a broom for the first time and it dragged me all the way around a mall. I couldn't control it at all, and I had no idea what was happening."

Tina laughed gently. "My first time on a broom was equally traumatizing. Someone paid a dragon to scare me off, to try and get me to leave town by making me fall off my broom when I was about a hundred feet in the air. Luckily, Sara managed to save me. That's how we got the swimming pool."

I gasped. "An actual, honest-to-goodness dragon?"

"Oh yes," Tina said, nodding. "They exist in the paranormal world. Although, they're shifters. They can easily take a human form as well. And to be fair to this dragon, he eventually apologized to me, and we're on good terms now. He's actually quite nice."

"Dragons," I muttered to myself, shaking my head. "I'm not sure I'd be able to handle dragons."

"Well, hopefully one day you will," Tina said. "I know your family is banished from the paranormal world right now, but you never know. A long time has passed since then, maybe Kaillie will be able to make an application to be let back in, or something. I don't really know how any of this stuff works, myself."

"Hopefully. That's the number one thing she wants in the world, to be able to go to the paranormal world and meet the rest of our coven. She loves her family, that's obvious, but she really wants to belong to that bigger group."

"I can understand that, I think," Tina said slowly. "It must be very frustrating to be denied access to a group you want to be a part of because of something someone else did."

"Yeah," I agreed. "Honestly, if there was something I could do to help her get there, I would do it. Kaillie has been so helpful. She's taught me most of the spells I know."

"I'm really glad you've got some nice people helping you," Tina said. "I'd give it a shot, but the spells I've learned are all from the coven of Jupiter."

"So if I tried them they wouldn't work?" I asked.

"They might work, but it would be more difficult, and they wouldn't act nearly as well as if you cast the same spell, but with the incantation that belongs to your coven."

"How many covens are there in the paranormal world?"

"Oh, goodness, dozens. At least. To be honest, I don't even know. Maybe even hundreds."

"Wow," I said. "That's so many more than I expected."

"There are a lot out there," Tina said. "More than I had expected at first, too. The paranormal world seems pretty small initially, compared to this one. But then, you get to realizing that it's a lot bigger than you think."

"Interesting," I replied, before stopping. "Ok, that should be it there. Ellie said it's a little red bungalow with a black roof." I pointed to a house about thirty feet back from the street, surrounded by woods.

Tina looked around. "It's fairly isolated, but this looks like the kind of place where if a nosy neighbor catches us sneaking around they're going to come at us with a shotgun."

"Yeah, I don't have great experiences with guns on this island," I replied. "Any chance you know a spell that can turn us invisible?"

Tina grinned. "That was one of the first ones I learned." She whipped out her wand and pointed it at me, and I gasped as I disappeared.

"You didn't say a spell," I said.

"You can say them in your head," Tina replied.

"Can you really? I was always told you have to say the spells."

"Most witches do. I should have thought of that and said the words, but I've taken to casting my spells silently and forgot; I just did that one out of habit."

"So how do you do it? Cast the spell without saying the words, I mean."

"Well, you need to still *think* the words. But if you think the words, and your intention and power as a witch is strong enough, the spell will still cast. It turned out I had some pretty powerful magical genes, so I manage it. Don't feel bad if you can't do it, though. Most witches can't. The only ones I know who can are myself and Amy."

"Ok," I said. "Well, you're up."

Tina pointed the wand at herself and a second later she disappeared as well. "Good. Now we can break and enter in peace."

"Hopefully with the help of magic it's just going to be 'enter' without the 'break'," I replied.

"I should be able to manage that," Tina said. The two of us made our way to the front door. This time, when Tina cast the spell, she muttered some words first, and I heard the deadbolt of the lock click open. We slipped into the house, closing the door quickly behind us. We were in.

CHAPTER 12

The inside of the bungalow looked like, well, what I imagined any house with a family of five, of which three were boys under six would look like. The entrance was littered with shoes, socks and jackets. To the right was a large living room, with toys scattered all around the carpet. To the left was a laundry room, with multiple baskets overflowing with clothes, some folded up nicely in the basket obviously ready to be taken back to the bedrooms, while others were evidently waiting to be washed and dried.

I moved deeper into the house to the kitchen, where plastic dishes and cutlery in all colors outnumbered the regular adult ones.

Down the hallway were three bedrooms. One of them was the master, Karen and Kyle's room, and the other for the boys, with the third being used as another playroom. I made my way into the master bedroom, calling out to Tina that was what I was doing.

"Cool, I'll take the living room," she replied.

The master bedroom was decently-sized, and in one corner was a small desk that held what appeared to be all of the family's important papers. I figured this was the place to be, and sat down, trying not to feel icky about the fact that I was about to rummage through someone else's personal information. After all, I was trying to find a killer. This was important.

The first folder I found contained all of the family's bank statements, and I looked through them carefully. After all, financial stress could cause a lot of strain on a relationship, and on a person. And while money was definitely tight for the family – they often only had around twenty or thirty dollars left in their bank account the day before Karen was paid – they did seem to be getting by. There were a couple of credit card statements, but none of them had more than a couple hundred dollars on the balance, and there were no statements for any large loans or anything of the sort. There hadn't been a car in the driveway, but I also didn't see any paperwork from a dealership, or any automatic payments coming out from their monthly accounts, so I assumed they owned their car free and clear.

Nothing in the financials seemed the least bit dodgy, so I looked around further. There was a laptop on the desk, and I opened it up. I groaned when I saw the password protection.

"Hey, Tina," I shouted towards the living room.

"Yeah?"

"How easy is it for a witch to unlock a computer's password?"

"Easy peasy," Tina replied. "Give me one second and I'll be right there."

I heard her footsteps coming down the hall, and a moment later she spoke.

"Jupiter, god of thunder, reveal the password of which we wonder."

I gasped as floating letters appeared above the laptop. *Kikikiki8686.* "Thanks," I grinned, typing the letters into the password field. The desktop burst to life, and I was in.

"No problem," Tina replied. "I haven't really found anything in the living room or the kitchen that might help us."

"Why don't you stay here and look through the laptop with me?" I suggested. "There might be a few more passwords we need to enter."

"Sure," Tina said, nodding. "Let me just go grab a chair from the kitchen."

A moment later a chair from the dining room began floating over, placed itself down on the floor next to mine, and the wood groaned slightly under Tina's weight as she sat down on it.

"Ok," I said. "Let's see what Karen was up to here."

Tina and I spent at least forty minutes going through all the files we could find on the computer, but it was all hunky-dory. Nothing seemed out of the ordinary at all. Most of the files were things a schoolteacher would print out for her students. We managed to log into her email account with some more magical help from Tina, but everything there looked normal as well. Just emails from parents thanking Karen for taking such good care of their children, asking about what time to come by for a meeting, that sort of thing.

"Wow, this lady led an impressively boring life," Tina said. "There doesn't seem to be a skeleton in any of the closets."

"Frankly, if I had three twin boys under the age of seven I'd probably be pretty boring too," I replied. "I imagine she doesn't have much time to do anything shady under the table."

"That's a good point," Tina replied. "Might as well check the trash, just in case."

I clicked on the icon for deleted emails, and Tina and I scanned through the list. Spam, spam, more spam, a couple of newsletters, but nothing strange.

"Hold on, what's that?" Tina asked suddenly.

"What's what?" I asked. "If you're pointing to it, I can't see."

"Whoops," Tina replied sheepishly. "I always forget that. The third one from the bottom, the appointment confirmation. What's that?"

My eyes scanned the page until they landed on the

email Tina mentioned. I clicked on it, and the screen popped open the email.

Karen had made an appointment for that Saturday, the day after she was stabbed, at two in the afternoon. An appointment with a law firm.

"McKinney and Associates," I read aloud. "Enchanted Enclave, Washington."

"Do you know who they are?" Tina asked.

"No, I haven't heard of them. Actually, I think I've seen a sign for their office, they're in one of the fancy buildings on Main Street, but I don't know what they do."

"Google them," Tina suggested, and I did exactly that.

"McKinney and Associates is a firm of experienced divorce, family law and personal injury attorneys who have been practicing in Washington State for over twenty-five years." I read aloud. "Wow. I wonder if Karen was considering getting a divorce."

"Now there's a reason to stab someone if I've ever heard one," Tina replied.

"No kidding," I muttered.

"Are there any other emails from the law firm?"

I typed in the email address in the search bar. "No, nothing."

"Well, there's a good lead to follow up on," Tina said. "What associate was Karen seeing?"

"Jean McKinney," I replied. "I'm guessing she won't

know a lot, but we might as well go and speak with her."

Before Tina had a chance to reply, however, a noise from the front door reached my ears. I instinctively looked over to where Tina was sitting, even though I couldn't see her.

"Hear that?" I asked in a hushed whisper.

"Yeah," she replied, her voice equally quiet. I quickly closed the computer programs and shut the lid, not entirely sure what to do. We could always go back out into the hallway to see what was going on, but then if whoever this was came into the hallway, we had limited options for not getting caught.

We could also just go out the window and into the backyard. This was my instinct, but at the same time, that meant we would never find out who was in this house. And frankly, a part of me suspected that if someone had just broken in, there was a reasonably good chance they were the person who had tried to murder Karen.

Of course, there was a chance that whoever had come in was allowed. It might have been Kyle returning home, or possibly Karen's parents arriving ahead of time. It might even have been a friendly neighbor who had been given a key checking in on things.

Tina grabbed me and pulled me towards the en suite bathroom. It was a good idea; an intruder was probably less likely to go into the bathroom than anywhere else in the house.

"Stupid idiot," I heard the person mutter as he made his way into the bedroom. "The stuff's got to be here somewhere."

Tina grabbed my arm gently as the intruder entered the bedroom. The two of us were standing in the middle of the bathroom, looking out into the bedroom as a man who looked to be in his late forties, with greying brown hair and a bit of a beer belly sticking out from his polo shirt and jeans looked furtively around.

Eventually, his eyes settled on the desk and he rushed over there, doing a much sloppier job than I had when it came to looking through the documents. Luckily, he didn't seem the least bit interested in the fact that there was a second chair at the desk. Instead of carefully having a look and putting everything back as he found it, the man simply tore through everything as fast as he could. He was obviously looking for something specific, and wasn't finding it.

Finally, he looked at the laptop. He looked around furtively, as though he was checking to make sure no one was watching him, then he unplugged the laptop and headed back out into the night.

When I heard the front door close behind him, I waited a solid fifteen, maybe twenty seconds before I finally spoke.

"Wow," was all I managed. My legs felt like jelly and my heart was beating at a million miles a minute.

"Yeah," Tina replied. "He just… took that laptop."

"I wonder what he wanted with it."

"Do you know who he was?"

I shook my head. "No. But then, if he wasn't a coffee shop regular, I wouldn't know him. I haven't lived here for long enough to get to know a lot of people. For all I know it could have been Kyle."

"It wasn't him," Tina replied. "There were a few pictures of the family in the living room. Kyle is thinner, with black hair. I don't know who that was, either."

"Ok, well, I suggest we get right on out of here in case one of the neighbors spotted this guy and decided to call the cops," I said. "Besides, I'm pretty sure we had a good look at everything."

"Right," Tina said.

The two of us left via the back door and headed back home. My heart was still racing from the scene we'd just seen. Who *was* the man who had been rummaging through Karen and Kyle's things? Was he the one who had stabbed her? The odds had to be pretty good.

CHAPTER 13

*T*wenty minutes later Tina and I were sitting in the living room, after having made it back home and fed Cleopawtra, who insisted that she'd been starving and that had it not been for my timely arrival she would have surely succumbed to a painful death.

Now she was happily munching away at her food in the kitchen while Tina and I enjoyed a glass of wine waiting for the others to appear.

"Why don't you show me one of the spells you've learned?" Tina suggested. "Just a simple one. No pressure, obviously. If you don't want to do it, then don't."

"No, it's a good idea, I need the practice," I replied, pulling out my wand. "*Saturn, god of plenty, make this lamp float with grace aplenty.*"

I pointed the wand at the floor lamp in the corner. It immediately began to hover about six inches off the ground, and as I waved my wand around the lamp followed. I made sure not to let it wander around too far; as it was still plugged in I figured things might end badly if the electrical cord got too taut. But after a moment I put it back down and dropped my wand, breaking the spell.

"Good job," Tina said with an approving nod. "That wasn't too shabby at all."

"Thanks," I said with a grin. "I still only know a handful of spells."

"Don't apologize for it," Tina replied. "No one should be expecting you to know more at this point. Yes, there's going to be a learning period where you're going to be catching up, and you're going to be far behind everyone else in your family, but you're also decades behind in terms of the time you've spent doing it. No one would expect you to be at an expert level right now. At least, nobody should be expecting you to be. Take your time to learn your skills properly without worrying about catching up. You're running your own race, and everyone started before you. You might not beat them to the finish line, but you'll get there eventually, and that's the most important thing – that you get there. You just have to do it, you don't have to do it on someone else's schedule."

"Ok," I said, feeling my confidence growing with every one of Tina's words. She was right. I had to focus on learning at my own speed, and to stop trying to take shortcuts and to try to catch up to Kaillie. I was going to get there. It might just take a bit longer than I was hoping for. "Let me try another one. This one I'm not completely sure about; I only learned it the other day."

"Go for it," Tina encouraged.

"Oh the weather outside is frightful, but the fire is so delightful. Saturn you're the god that makes things grow, let it snow, let it snow, let it snow."

I waved my hand around while Tina burst out laughing. A light dusting of snow began falling into the living room, seemingly from nowhere. I lifted my face to the ceiling, letting the light snowflakes fall and land on it.

"That spell is hilarious," Tina said.

"Well, I hope you know one to make the snow stop," I replied. "Because while I can make it snow, I cannot stop it from snowing, and so in a few minutes it's going to look like January in here instead of early May."

"That's not a problem," Tina replied, waving her wand around and muttering a spell herself. A moment later the snow disappeared, and Tina cast another quick spell to make the flakes that had landed dry up like they had never existed.

A moment later the front door opened, and the other four piled in.

"Ooh, wine," Ellie said, making a beeline for the kitchen.

"Don't be rude, Ellie," Tina chastised. "You're a guest, you have to ask if you can have some."

I laughed. "Help yourself," I said. "Glasses are in the second cupboard from the right."

Ellie pulled out her wand and muttered a spell, and a minute later four wine glasses flew down from the cupboard, landing in a perfect row on the kitchen counter, and she poured out one for everybody.

"So did you guys find out anything good?" Ellie asked.

"We have some potentially juicy information," I replied. "We were also interrupted by an intruder, though."

"Were you really?" Sara asked as she grabbed a glass from the counter and sat next to Tina on the couch. "Who was it?"

"We're not sure," I replied with a shrug. "He was maybe in his late forties, with greying brown hair, wearing a polo shirt."

"Oh, that sounds like Andrew," Ellie said. "He seemed pretty shaken up by the time Leanne and I finished interviewing him. That's a guy with something to hide."

"No wonder," Kaillie replied. "I should never have let the two of you go together. I bet Leanne steamrolled him completely."

"That sounds like Ellie, too. Alright, spill, what did you two do to him?" Sara asked.

"We didn't *do* anything," Ellie replied, crossing her arms. "We just asked him about Karen. It's not like we beat him to a pulp or hexed his face to turn into a pineapple or anything like that."

"Alright, well then why don't you tell us what you *did* ask him, and we can maybe figure out why he decided to make a beeline for Karen's house after speaking with you two," I said.

"Honestly, I have no idea why he did that," Leanne said. "We went to his place. I've known him for years, since he runs the rec center here. Basically everyone who grew up in Enchanted Enclave as a kid knows Andrew. So we knocked on his door. He was surprised to see us, but he invited us in."

"We jumped straight in when we got into the house, and we told him he had been seen arguing with Karen just a few days before she was stabbed. We told him that he had better tell us what they were arguing about before someone else found out about the argument and decided to tell Chief Jones," Ellie said. "He wasn't happy about that at all. He wanted to know who I was, and who had seen him arguing with Karen, but we refused to tell him. We said that we knew he was a good guy and would give him the benefit of the doubt if he told us what the argument was about."

"Then, he completely blew up on us," Leanne continued. "He told us that there was no argument, that whoever had told us that was lying. He insisted that he and Karen were on good terms, and that there was nothing between them that would have meant a fight.

He was so mad I was sure he was going to start throwing things, but in the end he just shouted at us to leave. We did, but I do think the man protests too much."

"Agreed," Ellie said. "On our way out we did see a car in the driveway, a silver Prius. We had a look at the seats inside, but there wasn't any blood or anything that might have indicated Karen was stabbed there."

"We should have thought to watch the house and follow him. Instead we went to the hospital to see if Karen had come back to town yet. We found out from one of the nurses that I went to school with that she should be coming back tomorrow morning, along with Kyle and the boys."

"That makes sense, they weren't at their house, and there was no car there to indicate they were on the island," I said. "I guess we'll have to sneak a look at Kyle's car tomorrow when he gets back."

"That's very interesting that Andrew went straight to Karen's house and stole her computer, though," Leanne said thoughtfully. "I wonder what he was after."

"He was definitely looking for something," Tina said. "He rummaged through all of her stuff. It sounds like he had a cursory glance at the living room, and then went straight for the bedroom. He went through the papers there really quickly, then grabbed the laptop and ran off."

"There were just credit card bills, bank statements, that sort of thing in the other papers that he left," I added. "So yeah, I don't know what he was looking for, but he must have guessed it was on the laptop."

"I'm surprised the cops haven't come by and taken it away, actually," Kaillie said thoughtfully. "You would think that with Karen having been stabbed they would have already gone through the house and taken anything that might be important."

"I bet that's Chief Jones' incompetence," Leanne replied. "It sounds like just the sort of thing he would do."

"Anyway," I interrupted, "before Andrew came and interrupted us, Tina and I did find something interesting on the laptop."

"Oh?" Sara asked.

"Karen had an appointment with a lawyer here on Enchanted Enclave scheduled for the day after she was stabbed. Jean McKinney."

Leanne's eyes widened. "She's a divorce lawyer."

"Is that it?" I asked. "The website seemed to indicate she did a few other things as well."

"The firm, as a whole, deals with other things. There are, I think, three lawyers that work there. With a place this small, you don't exactly need more than that. They run the gambit from personal injury to getting people's speeding tickets reduced to criminal activity, if needed. But Jean McKinney herself almost only does divorce and family law cases."

"So you'd say it's a pretty good bet that she was

going to see about getting a divorce?" I asked, and Leanne nodded.

"Yeah, Leanne is right," Kaillie confirmed. "Divorce and custody situations are what Jean *does*. She's basically the go-to in the entire San Juan Islands for anyone who's looking to get a divorce."

"Well, we were right," I said to Tina. "That certainly gives Kyle one heck of a motive if he wanted to get rid of his wife."

"What about Gary Vanderchuck?" I asked Kaillie and Sara. "Did you guys see him?"

"We did," Kaillie replied. "Gary takes his workouts very seriously. He was drinking a protein shake and beef jerky when he walked in, which is ridiculous since he wasn't even doing weights. He just finished eating then jumped right onto the treadmill. He wasn't pleased to see us. Sara and I each took one of the treadmills next to him. Of course, I'm pretty sure he thought Sara was a complete weirdo when she started ordering the machine around, telling it what speed to run at."

Tina snickered. "Now she knows how I felt my first time at a paranormal gym!"

"Wait, your treadmills are different?" I asked, then shook my head. "No, not now. You were saying?"

"Well, I finally figured out that you have to push *buttons* to make the treadmill work," Sara said. "It was so quaint, I've never seen anything like it. And there's no immersion capabilities either, so I think it would be quite boring to run on those for an hour or so."

"It definitely is," Leanne confirmed.

"Anyway, Gary initially seemed pretty pleased to have us running next to him, and was happy to strike up a conversation, until we asked him about Karen," Kaillie said. "Then he tried to shut it down pretty quickly."

"Kaillie mentioned the fact that it was well known he was in the middle of a big argument with Karen," Sara said. "He tried to deny it at first, and then we told him we had that information from multiple sources, and it was like he just gave up, you know? He turned off his treadmill and said he wasn't going to talk about it there."

"So we went out into one of the studios that wasn't being used," Kaillie continued. "He asked us why we wanted to know about Karen, and I told him the truth. I said Leanne was the one that hit her, and that the very least she could do for Karen was to find the person who tried to kill her, and that Sara and I were helping her to do that."

"Gary looked at us for a while, as if he was trying to tell if Kaillie was lying to him, and eventually I guess he decided she was telling the truth, because he started talking. He told us that yes, it was true that he and Karen had disagreed about the way under-performing students should be treated, and that their discussions had gotten heated, but he said that overall, we had it all wrong," Sara said.

"Oh?" I asked.

"He said that he actually loved the fact that Karen had so much passion and determination, and that he wished there were more teachers out there like her," Sara continued. "He said that even though they disagreed on this particular topic, the fact that she fought for her students and fought for what she believed in was the most important thing to him, and he hoped more than anything that she was going to be ok."

"Did you believe him?" I asked, and Kaillie nodded.

"I mean, I did, initially. But of course, I wasn't *just* going to take his word for it. So we asked him where he was the night Karen was stabbed. It turns out Gary wasn't even on the island. He was on the mainland in Seattle for some sort of school administrator's conference. He told us if we didn't believe him we could ask his wife; she was at home the whole time and he wasn't."

"Oh," I replied. "Well, that eliminates him as a suspect, I guess."

"I think so," Sara replied. "Plus, we asked him what he was driving, and on our way back out, we looked at the inside of his car, just in case. A green Corolla. Sure enough, there was no sign of blood or anything to indicate that Karen was stabbed in it."

"We need to get a look at Kyle's car," I said.

"We do," Leanne confirmed.

"Well, we'll leave you to it, as we do need to get back to Western Woods and we have a bit of a trip ahead of us," Tina said, standing up. "I hope you don't feel as though we intruded here."

"No, not at all," I replied warmly. "Thank you for coming. You have no idea how much your advice and wisdom has helped me. I'm really grateful that you were willing to take the time to come here."

"Not a problem," Ellie replied. "We don't come to the human world enough. It's fun here, in a quaint way. I bet this would make a great holiday destination, one where we can relax and just leave our wands at home."

"Yeah, that sounds nice," Sara said, nodding. "Although I don't like the treadmills here."

"Don't worry, neither do I," I replied with a laugh.

"Let us know what happens with the investigation," Ellie said.

"Will it work if we call you?" I asked, and Sara nodded.

"It certainly should. Let's swap numbers and we can stay in touch."

"Good idea," Tina said, and the six of us spent a few minutes making sure we all had each other's' numbers.

"If you meet anyone important, you could suggest to them that our family doesn't deserve its exile anymore," Kaillie said. "We'd really appreciate it."

"The odds are low – Western Woods isn't really an important town and we don't get many visitors from high up, but if we get the chance, we'll do it," Tina promised. "Hopefully we'll get to see you in the paranormal world sometime."

"I hope so," Kaillie replied earnestly.

"In the meantime, thanks again for coming," I said. "You have no idea how much your words have helped me."

"I'm just glad I was able to help," Tina replied. "You keep doing what you're doing. Keep being yourself."

I nodded and gave Tina a hug. "Take care of yourself."

"You too."

A few minutes later the Western Woods witches left, leaving the three of us in the living room on our own once more.

CHAPTER 14

"*I*'m really not sure this is going to work," I said the next day as I got dressed in the fanciest clothes I owned – a blouse and a pair of slacks that I had bought for my job as a receptionist.

"Don't worry, it'll be fine," Leanne said. "We need to confirm that Karen was going to see Jean McKinney about a divorce, and there's no other way to do it except to go into the office."

"Yeah, but why do *I* have to be the one to pretend that I have a long-lost husband who no one can find?"

"Because literally everyone in town knows Kaillie and me. No one knows you, though."

"Yeah, but won't everyone find out about this if that's what I tell the lawyer?"

"That's what client confidentiality is for," Leanne replied. "Your lawyer isn't allowed to tell anybody anything you've told them, so no, your secret will be safe."

"It's not a secret, it's a lie."

"Po-tay-to, po-tah-to."

"You know, the more time I spend with you, the more I'm starting to understand why Kaillie has the reputation of being the good one in the family."

"Yeah, that's probably fair enough. Now come on, let's do this."

Leanne and I walked into the office on the ground floor of one of the commercial buildings on Main Street. It was plainly decorated, basically exactly what I would have expected from a small, generalist law firm. The walls were beige, the furniture simple and obviously inexpensive. When we walked in, a receptionist with curly brown hair who looked to be in her early forties looked up at us.

"Hello, do you have an appointment?" she asked.

"Yes, my cousin here made one this morning," Leanne replied. "She needs to see Jean for an initial consult. Eliza Emory."

"Of course," the receptionist said, all business. "Please have a seat, and we'll call Mrs. Emory up shortly."

Eliza and I sat down in the waiting area, joining a man who held a manila folder full of documents close to his chest, as if he were worried that if he released his grip on the files at all they'd vanish into thin air.

I probably looked just as nervous as the man was. I wasn't a good liar. Actually, scratch that. I was a *terrible* liar. I didn't like misleading people, but Leanne was right. We needed to get as much information as we could. It could really prove that Kyle had the perfect motive to try and kill his wife, especially given as her appointment was the day after she was stabbed.

The receptionist called the man in after about three or four minutes, and then five minutes after that, she called my name.

I stood up, Leanne flashed me a confident smile and gave me a thumbs up, and motioned for me to get in there.

I followed the receptionist through a short hallway, and she led me into a decently-sized office occupied by a woman in her fifties, with her grey hair tied back into a bun, her glasses reflecting the screen of the computer she stared at. As soon as she heard me enter, Jean McKinnie looked up and gave me a warm smile.

"Hello, you must be Eliza."

"That's me," I said quietly.

"I'm Jean. Please, have a seat."

I did as she asked, carefully sinking into the comfortable chair across from her desk.

"So," Jean started, wasting no time. "What can I do for you today?"

"Well," I started, stammering slightly. "See, I'm new in town. I come from San Francisco. And the thing is, when I lived there, I was married. I left him, but we're not divorced."

"And you'd like to take care of the paperwork?" Jean asked. I nodded. "Well, that's not a problem at all. I've been doing divorces for years. What kind of assets do you have?"

"Ummm... nothing, really."

"No house? Either separate or between you?"

"No."

"What about kids?"

"Definitely not!"

That earned a smile from Jean. "Good. That will make things easier. Were either one of you cheating on the other?"

"Errmmm... no," I finally managed to stammer. Boy, I was really not good at this whole lying thing. Then, I interrupted, since I needed to get the conversation to Karen. "My friend Karen referred me here, you know. She was supposed to have an appointment here the other day."

Jean made a non-committal noise in her throat. She wasn't opening up at all, so I tried again. "Did you hear about what happened to Karen? She was stabbed. Did she ever make it in to see you?"

Jean looked at me carefully. "I'm afraid I cannot talk about current clients, or in any way confirm or deny that Karen was even a client of mine."

I sighed, and Jean looked at me carefully. "What are you, really? A reporter? You're not married, are you?"

Great. She had seen straight through me, and I'd barely even done anything. I really was a bad liar.

"No, I'm not a reporter," I replied. I decided to go with the truth. After all, lies hadn't gotten me anywhere so far. "My cousin Leanne and I were the ones who found Karen when she was stabbed. Leanne feels terribly because she hit Karen with her car slightly when Karen ran out into the road to flag us down, and we decided that we want to try and find the person who hurt her, especially with her coming into town. We know that she had an appointment scheduled with you for the day after she was stabbed, but it doesn't say what about. Her husband Kyle is one of our main suspects, and I was hoping you'd be able to tell us what she was meeting you for."

A smile flittered across Jean's lips, which surprised me. "Well, that's not the strangest story I've ever heard."

"Really? It's not?" I was honestly surprised. Jean took the complete change of face super well considering she had been expecting a client who wanted a divorce from her estranged husband, not a client who was looking for information to solve a stabbing.

"I've been practicing law on this island for nearly thirty years. You wouldn't believe the things I've seen. I've had to go to court in front of a judge and argue that it be stated in the divorce agreement that my client's ex-wife wasn't allowed to teach their parrot to insult him. I've walked in on my client and her ex doing it on the conference room table during a break in depositions. This change in conversation doesn't even make the top ten list of weird things to happen *this year*, and it's not even summer yet."

"Well, in that case, can you help me?" I asked.

"Sorry," Jean said with a shrug. "Regardless of your reasons, I still can't tell you anything about Karen's case. That would be a huge breach of confidentiality."

I frowned slightly. "Can you at least tell me if she was here to discuss something about her husband?"

"I'm afraid I can't say one way or the other," Jean said, holding her hands out in apology.

"Alright, thanks," I said dejectedly, getting up from my seat.

"If you ever do find yourself in need of a divorce attorney, please come and see me again," Jean said as I left. I nodded and made my way back to the waiting room, where I made a thumbs down motion to Leanne as I headed towards her. She frowned as she stood up and made her way towards me.

"So it didn't go well?"

I shook my head. "Wouldn't tell me anything."

"Alright," Leanne said. "Well, it was worth a shot."

The two of us left the law firm and went back out into the street, where we almost immediately ran into Aunt Lucy.

"Where are the rest of the Floozies?" Leanne asked.

"Busy with stuff," Aunt Lucy said. "So I thought I'd find my favorite nieces and see how their investigation into a murder is going."

"Badly," Leanne admitted. "We know Karen had an appointment with Jean, but she won't tell us anything about it. We want confirmation that it was about a divorce. I'd like to have a look at that computer, but the receptionist is glued to that chair."

Aunt Lucy grinned, and I had a bad feeling about what was about to happen.

"Go back in there and ask her something," Aunt Lucy said. "I'll take care of the rest."

"Would Kaillie be ok with what you're about to do?" I asked cautiously.

"Kaillie is never ok with anything I do," Aunt Lucy replied. "That doesn't mean it's not fun."

"Fun wasn't what I was worried about," I muttered as Leanne grabbed me and dragged me back towards the law office. We went back inside and the receptionist looked at us once more.

"Yes?" she asked.

"Sorry, I was just wondering if you have a business card for Jean," Leanne said smoothly. "I have an aunt who is looking into getting an attorney, and I wanted to recommend her."

"Of course," the receptionist said, leaning over and grabbing a card from a pile on the desk and handing it to Leanne.

Just then, there came a rumbling from outside. I spun around just in time to see a sinkhole open up in the middle of the street. A late-model blue sedan was headed towards it, and must not have seen it in time, because it drove right into the hole, falling about three feet with a huge clang.

CHAPTER 15

"My goodness!" the receptionist said, jumping up from her chair and rushing out into the street. I stood, glued to the spot, horrified while Leanne immediately jumped into action. She ran to the receptionist's desk and began typing away while I eventually regained my senses and followed the receptionist out into the street to see if there was anything I could do to help.

I stopped short when I saw who was in the car: it was Ariadne Stewart, the cantankerous owner of one of the local gift shops and the woman who had a feud with Aunt Lucy going back decades.

She had gotten out of the car now and was standing in the bottom of the sinkhole, surrounded by concrete.

"I know this was you, Lucy!" she shouted out as people tried to get down into the hole to help her out.

Her hands were on her hips as she yelled. "I know it was you!"

"Hold on, Ariadne," Aunt Lucy called down. "You must have hit your head in that crash. People are coming down to help you. Just wait for them, ok?"

"You always were catty," Ariadne replied. "Don't you know how much this car costs? Of course you don't; you haven't worked a day in your life. You always were a lazy piece of crap. Well, let me tell you, this car is worth more than anything you own, and I swear I'm sending you the bill for repairs."

"I'm fairly certain no body shop is going to believe that I have the ability to create sinkholes, as much as I consider it a compliment," Aunt Lucy replied calmly. "I may be clever, but altering the island's geology is beyond even my own skills."

Ariadne seethed, stomping her feet on the ground. "You would resent me for being so successful. It's not my fault you've failed at everything you ever tried. But that's no reason to take it out on my beautiful new car."

"Listen to what you're saying, Ariadne," Aunt Lucy replied, shaking her head. "I think we're going to need an ambulance here. She might have a concussion," she called out.

At that point, a couple of men managed to climb down and reach Ariadne.

"Are you alright, ma'am?" one of them asked, reaching towards her, and she moved her arm away.

"Of course I'm not alright! My poor car has been completely destroyed!"

Destroyed was probably a bit of an overreaction. To be honest, it looked in pretty good shape considering it had fallen about three feet into a hole. There was a dent on the front right bumper, and the left panel seemed to have been scratched up by a piece of loose concrete, but apart from that the car looked pretty much fine. I was fairly certain a body shop wouldn't have too much problem restoring it right back to new.

"Your car is just a car," the man replied. "There's an ambulance on its way to take care of you."

"*Just* a car?" Ariadne screeched. "It's not *just* a car. This car is the reward I get for being a job creator in this town. I deserve it for everything I do for people. But I couldn't expect you to understand. I bet you're just a laborer or something. People like you, who aren't actually successful at anything, wouldn't know real success if it hit you in the face."

"You know, maybe you should just wait for the EMTs if you want help getting out of this hole," the man muttered, taking a step back and heading back out to street level.

"What, you're just going to leave an old lady like me stranded here?" Ariadne harrumphed, her hands on her hips.

"Some life advice: don't be mean to people trying to help you," Aunt Lucy called down. "It might go a bit better for you."

"Why don't you just keep your opinions to yourself up there?" Ariadne called back.

A minute later an ambulance pulled up to the hole, with the crowd of people that had gathered around moving to make space for it to reach. The professionals sprang into action and I realized I'd completely forgotten about Leanne and the receptionist. I looked around to find the receptionist still standing on the edge of the hole, watching in awe as the scene unfolded. I dared to glance inside the office to find Leanne just making her way towards the door. A moment later she sidled up next to me.

"Have I missed anything fun?"

"Just Ariadne blaming Aunt Lucy for creating the sinkhole."

"Well, she's not wrong."

"That's true. We're the only ones who know that, though. Everyone else thinks Ariadne is insane. She then insulted the man trying to help her."

"That sounds about right."

"Did you find out anything on the computer?"

Leanne nodded. "Yes. There were a couple of notes in the file on Karen's appointment. She was definitely seeing Jean about getting a divorce from Kyle, and there was a note about gambling debts."

"Gambling debts?" I asked, my eyebrows rising.

"Yeah. That's all it said. I guess maybe Kyle was addicted or something, and my guess is that was why Karen wanted to leave him."

"Wow," I said, watching as Ariadne insisted on being loaded up onto the stretcher and taken to the hospital, and telling everyone within earshot that she would be suing Aunt Lucy for doing this to her. "I'm surprised. I would have thought we'd have seen some sort of evidence of it in the financial documents."

Leanne shrugged. "My guess is Kyle had his own secret set of accounts. Or maybe he was selling some family jewelry for cash, something like that. The sort of thing that doesn't show up on ordinary financial documents."

"I guess so," I said. "Well, that makes him our prime suspect as far as I'm concerned."

"Agreed," Leanne replied. "Although I also still want to know what the argument between Karen and Andrew was about."

"Right," I said. "We need to get a look at Kyle's car as well. They should be back this evening. My guess is he'll be parked at the hospital."

"I think so," Leanne said. "I know his car. It's a black truck; he keeps all his work stuff in it. Karen drives a blue Honda."

"We should check them both, just to be safe. Neither car was at the house the other day."

"That's true," Leanne said. "Maybe she left it at the school."

The ambulance doors closed just then, with Ariadne being driven off to the hospital, and Aunt Lucy came towards us.

"Was that enough of a distraction for you?" she asked.

"That was perfect," Leanne replied.

Aunt Lucy cackled. "I was just going to set a tree on fire or something, but then I saw Ariadne driving down the street and I just couldn't help myself. Of course, she shouldn't have her license anyway. They should have taken it from her years ago. She's blind as a bat, she doesn't look where she's going, and she has the reflexes of a snail that's smoked a little too much pot. She was a good thirty, forty feet from the sinkhole when it opened and she *still* didn't manage to stop in time, even though she was going ten miles an hour, tops."

"She doesn't know you're a witch though, right?" I asked. "After all, she was blaming you for what happened."

"That's because blaming others is easier than blaming her own terrible driving," Aunt Lucy replied. I didn't point out that it *was* Aunt Lucy's fault that the sinkhole opened in the first place. "The only reason she bought that new car is because she drove the old one onto the beach and straight into the water last summer. She claimed someone moved the signs for the parking lot so she thought she was still on the road, and that because it was foggy she didn't see the water until it was too late."

"Of course, it was a perfectly sunny day out," Leanne said to me. "And no one else saw that fog except for Ariadne. Everyone else knew she was driving into the ocean. She even ran over a kid's sandcastle on the way there. The only reason she didn't drown was because the lifeguard on duty ran in and managed to save her."

"Wow," I said. "That's crazy!"

"She tried to sue the county for moving the signs, but obviously it didn't work," Aunt Lucy said. "I'm sure I'm going to be named in a suit. I guess if any one of us needs a lawyer right now, it's going to be me. Ah well, it was completely worth it."

I laughed as Leanne and I left Aunt Lucy and made our way back down the street.

CHAPTER 16

The two of us decided to walk towards the school. After all, Karen's car hadn't turned up. Maybe that was the car she had been in when she was stabbed, but maybe not. We ended up reaching the parking lot around noon, and the sound of children shrieking and laughing as they played outside reached our ears long before the single-story brick building came into view.

At the front of the building was a small parking lot, and sure enough, in one of the spots about thirty feet from the front door was a blue Civic.

"That's got to be it, right?" I asked Leanne, who nodded.

"Yeah, surely."

The two of us made our way up to the car and peeked inside. Sure enough, it was a regular Civic interior. No blood or anything of the sort on the seats. No sign of any stains having been recently cleaned, either. Three booster seats in the back. The fact that the car was still sitting here in the parking lot indicated to me that Karen had left the school without her car.

"There's Gary's green Corolla," I said, looking at the other cars in the lot. It was parked next to Karen's Civic. It looked to be about five years old, with a number of bumper stickers on the back: protect our winters, meat is murder, stop drunk driving and love is love. I peered inside to see the seats looking completely normal. It was a tan interior, too, so it wasn't like it would be possible to hide the blood, and a couple of old stains in the fabric proved that Gary Vanderchuck hadn't gotten the upholstery changed in the last couple of days, either.

Between that and the fact that he was apparently at a conference in Seattle the night Karen was stabbed, I was pretty much ready to write him off completely as a suspect.

"Excuse me," a voice said a moment later, and I looked up, startled. The man walking towards us was tall, of medium weight, wearing a polo shirt and slacks and walking with the confidence and authority of someone who was used to being in charge. "What are you doing near my car?"

"Mr. Vanderchuck," Leanne said, and as soon as he saw my cousin his expression changed.

"Leanne Stevens," he replied. "It's been quite a few years since I've seen you, but given as I saw your cousin just the other day, I assume you're here for the same reason?"

"More or less," Leanne confirmed. "We were just checking to see if Karen's car was still here."

"Yes, it's been here in the lot since I got back," Gary confirmed. "I heard she's being brought back to the island this afternoon. I'm so glad she's going to be alright."

"We are too," I said. "You said you were in Seattle for a conference when she was stabbed?"

"Yes," Gary replied. "I can't believe anyone would do something like this to a woman like Karen. As I told Kaillie and her friend, we might have had disagreements about how to treat the children, but the reality was she cared a lot about her students, and that's the most important thing."

"Who do you think might have done this to her?" I asked, and Gary shrugged.

"I couldn't tell you. I can't believe anyone would have such a grudge against Karen that they would try to kill her."

"Do you know how her family life was going?" Leanne asked.

"We weren't that close," Gary replied. "Sorry."

"Do you know anything about gambling in town? Anyone involved in it?" Leanne asked, and Gary frowned.

"Gambling? No, I've never heard of any happening here. I mean, I'm sure people do it on the internet and stuff, but that's all. Why?"

"No real reason," Leanne replied. "Just something we heard."

"Well, I can't say I know anything about that."

"Alright, thanks," I said, and Leanne and I left, the bell sounding a few minutes later to let the kids know their lunch break was over and that it was time to head back into class.

"Did you see the inside of the car? Kaillie and Sara already said it looked fine."

"Yeah, and it does," I confirmed. "It doesn't look new, either. What about Andrew?"

"He should be at the recreation center now," Leanne said. "After all, it's a weekday. I don't think we should bother him, though. He seemed pretty nervous about talking the other night, and I think we might get more out of him if we spy on him instead."

"Spy on him?" I asked, my eyes widening.

"That's right. Do you want to learn how to cast the spell that lets you eavesdrop on people?" Leanne asked with a grin. "I heard Aunt Lucy cast it so many times in my life even I know the incantation for it."

"I don't know," I said carefully. "I'm not sure I'll be able to do it."

"Well, if it doesn't work we can always text Aunt Lucy and ask her to do it for us," Leanne offered. "But consider this your magical lesson for the day."

"What if something messes up?" I asked, thinking about what Tina told me. It wasn't easy to say, but I took a deep breath and continued. "It's not like you're going to be able to reverse it. I think right now I'm better off practicing where it can't hurt me."

Leanne nodded. "Ok, that's totally cool. If you're not comfortable with it that's fine, I'll text Aunt Lucy. She'll help us. I don't want to push you into something you're uncomfortable with."

"Thanks," I replied, a wave of gratefulness washing over me. Tina had been right when she had told me to trust the people around me. I wasn't comfortable with using magic in public yet, and rather than pressure me to do it, Leanne had completely understood.

I really did need to learn to trust more. Leanne had already saved my life. And she had just proven that she was completely comfortable going at my pace when it came to learning magic. I had grown up with just Dad and myself, and I still found it so difficult to trust others. But Tina had told me to rely on the people I was close to now, and time and time again, they came through for me.

"No problem," Leanne said, pulling out her phone and typing away. To be completely honest, I wasn't totally sold on the idea of inviting Aunt Lucy. Leanne seemed completely fine with her brand of chaos, but one person had already been taken away in an ambulance because of her today. Even if she did seem completely fine.

Maybe Kaillie had a point about the fact that we needed to be better witches to be invited back into the paranormal world. On the other hand, there were no guarantees that would ever happen even if we *were* good, and surely solving an attempted murder would be more important than casting a few erratic spells that negatively affected Aunt Lucy's worst enemy.

"She's coming, she'll meet us there," Leanne told me, leading me away from the school. I had yet to visit the Enchanted Enclave recreation center, and it turned out to be on one of the side streets off Main Street, not far from the center of town. The building featured a pool, a gym, some squash courts and a basketball court as well as a few diverse community rooms. It was nice that even a small place like Enchanted Enclave could have somewhere like this for kids – and adults for that matter – to get some exercise in, especially when the weather turned ugly.

When we walked in, Aunt Lucy was sitting at a plastic table near the small concession stand, eating fries from a cardboard container. She waved us over when she saw us, and the two of us made our way over, sitting in the plastic chairs across from her. Leanne grabbed a fry from the container and munched down on it.

"We need you to cast a spell for us," Leanne explained to our aunt.

"Is that all I am to you? A vessel through which to perform magic?"

"You also take my side whenever I'm arguing with dad," Leanne replied. "Most of the time, anyway."

"That is true. What spell do you need?"

"We want to eavesdrop on Andrew," Leanne said. "Have you seen him?"

"He walked to his office about five minutes ago," Aunt Lucy said.

"Perfect," I replied.

Aunt Lucy pulled her wand from her purse and pointed it towards a door to our left, making sure to keep it under the table so that no one nearby could see it. Leanne put a hand on Aunt Lucy's arm and motioned for me to do the same, which I did.

"*Saturn, god of plenty, enhance Andrew's voice and make it loud as a banshee,*" Aunt Lucy muttered. A second later I gasped. I could hear a man's voice inside my head; it was like he was standing right there next to me.

"No, you don't have to worry about it. It's all taken care of," the man said.

"That's Andrew," Leanne mouthed at me from the other end of the table, and I nodded.

There was a pause, and the man spoke again. "Look, I know you think she's going to tell everyone what she knows, but I'm telling you, it's not a problem anymore. Karen has way more important things to deal with now. We're a low priority. You don't need to do anything. But I'm telling you, I'm out. I can't do it anymore."

This time, the three of us exchanged glances. I had suspected Andrew was talking about Karen, but now there wasn't a shadow of a doubt.

"Look, she's in the hospital. Goodness knows how long she's going to be there. She's supposed to pull through, but you never know with medical stuff. I had an aunt with pneumonia a few years back. The doctors told us she was going to pull through, that she was going to make it, then bam. One day, her heart just gave out. You never know. So no, I'm not going to do anything about it right now. I'm going to let it play its course. We're not in any trouble right now. I'm telling you."

There was another pause. "Fine. Do that. But if anyone comes to you asking questions, you clam up, ok? I've already got those meddling women from that coffee company coming around asking me about Karen. Like they've got any right. But they don't know squat, don't worry. They're just snooping. They're nothing we need to bother with."

My veins turned to ice as I heard those words. Sure, we might have been 'nothing to bother with' right now, but I couldn't help but feel a little bit worried. Who was Andrew on the phone with? What if that person decided that we *were* trouble and decided they were going to do something about it?

"Right," Andrew continued after another pause. "We need to just keep acting like nothing's happening. Besides, I'm telling you, the cops up here are idiots. They're not going to catch on. It's been a year, and they still don't have a clue that we're doing it. Leave the Karen situation to me. She's not going to be a problem,

I'm telling you. But I can't keep doing this. It's too much pressure. There's going to be an investigation, and I can't get caught, you got me?"

There was silence for a couple of minutes, and then Andrew started muttering to himself. "I swear, I should never have done it. Why I thought I could get out of things this easily…" His voice trailed off, and a minute later the door Aunt Lucy had pointed the wand at opened up, and a short, stout man with a thick black beard walked out, looking at the ground, obviously wrapped up in his own thoughts.

"Well, that was certainly more enlightening than I was expecting," Aunt Lucy said. "It sounds like Andrew is mixed up in something he shouldn't be."

"I want to know who he was on the phone with," Leanne said. "Hopefully it was his cell phone so that would mean there's a record of it. Although, we'd still have to get access to the phone to look at those records."

"That's very easily stolen," Aunt Lucy said. "I can cause another distraction and then Eliza can cast a spell to make his phone float over here."

"No, Eliza doesn't want to use magic in public until she gets the hang of it a bit more," Leanne explained. I had honestly expected Aunt Lucy to fight that a little bit, but she just shrugged.

"Alright, well, no rush in teaching her spells I guess. It's not like it matters that she's behind the rest of us when we're among the only five witches in this world who can use magic at all. How are you going to get his phone, then?"

"I don't know," Leanne admitted. "Maybe that's a problem for the future. If Karen is back in town, I'd like to go and see her. Although, I don't know if she'll see me."

"Alright, well, I'll leave you to it then. Carmen says Carolyn Doyle is getting her hair dyed blue, and we all want to see how it turns out, so I made an appointment at the salon at the same time, and have to get going. I'll show you pictures tonight. A teenager showed me how to take selfies to spy on people without them noticing the other day, so I'm going to try that out."

Aunt Lucy waved and walked off, and Leanne shook her head.

"Who's Carolyn Doyle?" I asked.

"A woman Aunt Lucy went to school with. They didn't get along in high school, and have had a low-key rivalry ever since. Nothing like Aunt Lucy and Ariadne though. That feud is a whole other level of crazy. It's best to stay out of it."

"Fair enough," I replied. "Let's go to the hospital and see if Karen wants to see you, or if she's happy to pretend you never existed."

Given the look on her face, Leanne was very worried about the second option being reality.

CHAPTER 17

"*L*ook, I'm sure it'll be fine," I said for what felt like the millionth time during the ten minute walk from the recreation center to the hospital. "She ran into the car looking for help, and you did your best to avoid her, and then you saved her life. That has to count for something."

"It probably would have counted for more if I hadn't hit her at all," Leanne said with a sigh. "I wouldn't blame her if she absolutely hated me. Come on, we have to stop at the florist first. I can't show up empty-handed."

The Enchanted Enclave florist was on Main Street, a small shop absolutely teeming with green life. As we walked in, a woman behind the counter smiled at us as she trimmed the leaves off some long-stemmed roses. Her long red hair flowed down to her waist, and her light brown eyes were friendly and warm. She looked exactly like what I imagined a fairy who lived in the woods among the trees and moss would look like, and here in the middle of a store surrounded by plants she looked in her element.

"Hello there," she greeted us in a soft voice. "How can I help you?"

"Hi," Leanne said. "I'm looking for a simple bouquet of flowers to give to someone."

"Do you have an occasion in mind?" the woman asked. "I can definitely help you."

"It's kind of a sympathy thing."

I had to smile at the idea that the florist had a whole section of "sorry I hit you with my car" flowers just sitting around.

"Alright, I can help you with that," the florist said, nodding as she made her way to the wall on the left, which was lined with buckets with various flowers. "If this is for someone to get better, I like to go with happy, hope-inducing color combinations, like purple and yellow. Look at these daisies, for example. Don't you think they'd go well with these peonies?"

"Yeah, I do," Leanne said. "That's perfect."

"Excellent. And what price range were you looking at? I can make you a custom bouquet based on that."

"Um, I don't know," Leanne said. "What do people normally spend on someone who they hope gets well soon but that they didn't know, when it's their fault they found themselves in that situation?"

The florist raised her eyebrows. "You're giving these flowers to Karen, aren't you?"

Leanne groaned. "Great. So word has gotten around town that I'm the one who hit her, hasn't it?"

"I'm afraid so," the florist replied with an apologetic look. "Although, if it's any consolation, I've also heard that it was thanks to you that she's still alive. And I am glad Karen is ok."

"Did you know her well?" I asked, and the florist shrugged.

"I wouldn't say *well*, but I did know her. I work as a substitute teacher sometimes when the florist shop is closed, and my brother Gary is the principal at the school. Still, I saw her as a coworker more than I did as a florist."

"Did she ever talk to you about her husband?" Leanne asked, and the woman's eyes widened.

"Kyle? You can't possibly think *he* would have done it, do you? Well, I suppose anything is possible. You never really do know people, do you? I always thought they were a loving couple. In fact, I still do."

"That may very well be true, we're not really looking into it or anything," I said hurriedly.

"Oh no, of course not," the woman said. "I can't say I really did hear Karen speak about her husband very much. She'd mention his work from time to time, but she really preferred to speak about her little boys. She's very dedicated to them, you know. And they're such little darlings. Of course, they can be a handful. But then, that's what children are, aren't they? And Karen was so good with them. She would work a full day at school and then still take them to soccer practice and have oranges sliced up for all the kids when they were finished. I honestly don't know how she does it. I don't have kids and I always end up completely wiped after I do a day of teaching."

"I just can't imagine who would have done this to her," Leanne said, shaking her head.

"Neither can I," the woman replied. "She was just so nice to everyone. The last person you'd ever think would be murdered. Anyway, to answer your question, I think thirty dollars would be a fine budget for someone in your situation."

"Alright, well, let's round it up and make it forty then," Leanne said. "I really do feel bad for not getting out of the way in time."

The florist gave Leanne a sympathetic look. "I'm sure Karen will understand. The universe obviously willed for everything to happen as it did, and as a result Karen is still with us and alive. I was thrilled to hear she's coming back to recuperate here. You know, I know a lot of people consider it to be pseudo-science, but I really believe there is something to the notion that you recover better in the place you call home."

"I can believe that," Leanne said. "After all, when you're really, truly home there's a sense of belonging, a relaxation that you don't get when you're elsewhere. Even Seattle is close to here, but it's not Enchanted

Enclave. It's not home for Karen. I imagine she will have an easier time being able to relax and recover when she knows she's here."

"I do hope so," I chimed in. "Her parents will be there too, at least. They're helping with the boys, I assume."

"Yes, it can't have been easy for Karen, taking care of her home and of her children," the florist said. "She handled her responsibilities so well, but there is a saying that just because someone bears a weight well doesn't mean it's heavy. I admire Karen for how she carried the weight she bore. She did not deserve this."

As she spoke, the florist put together a small bouquet of flowers, which she then handed to Leanne. "I'm sure she will speak with you."

"Thanks," Leanne replied. "I hope so."

We left the florist and made our way to the small hospital. Leanne clutched the flowers to her chest, and the color drained from her face as we approached.

"It's going to be fine," I told her, but my cousin just nodded in reply.

The few times I had been to a hospital in my life, it had been fairly chaotic. The emergency room had been full of people with various ailments, from a little boy yelling that his ear hurt, to a teenager curled up into a ball on the chair and rocking herself back and forth, and an old woman yelling at the nurses that she'd been waiting two hours and needed to be seen *now*.

Enchanted Enclave's hospital was a different situation entirely. The waiting room consisted of about five chairs lined up against the wall near the reception desk, where a nurse was comfortably tapping away at a computer. Only one of the chairs was occupied, by an older man casually drinking a coffee who I suspected was simply visiting someone and not actually waiting to be seen.

Standing to one side, near a rack of brochures offering information about a number of common diseases was Detective Ross Andrews. He was flipping through his notebook, but as soon as he glanced up and saw us he strode over to where Leanne and I were standing as we waited for the nurse at the reception area.

"Hello, Eliza. Leanne."

"Hi, Detective," I said. "So it's true that Karen is here again?"

"That's her father there," he replied, motioning his head towards the man with the cup of coffee. "They moved her over here an hour ago and the rest of the family has just gone home to get some rest. Her father insisted that someone should stay here at the hospital just in case."

Just then Detective Andrews' phone rang, and he motioned for us to hold on as he took a few steps away from us to answer it. His face immediately went dark; the family must have gotten home and found out about the break in.

"Alright, I'll be right there," he said, hanging up the

phone, and turned to us. "I wanted to speak with the two of you, but it's going to have to wait. Excuse me." With that, he strode out of the hospital.

"I guess we can't tell him we know it was Andrew who broke in," I muttered to Leanne, who shook her head.

"Nope. Far too many questions we don't want to answer if we do. That one's going to be up to him to solve. On the bright side, Detective Andrews isn't a total idiot like our chief of police, so there's a chance he might actually find the culprit on his own."

We could always hope, especially since I was fairly certain Andrew was the killer.

CHAPTER 18

The nurse at the reception counter was initially a little bit frosty with her reception, until she learned that Leanne was the one who had found Karen and that she wanted to make sure she was alright. Eventually, the nurse relented, and told us that as long as she came with us and asked Karen if she wanted to speak with us first, it would be fine for us to see her.

Leanne didn't say a word as we followed the nurse down the hallway. She eventually stopped in front of a private room and motioned for us to wait outside, which we did. A moment later, the nurse came back out, smiling. "She's more than happy to have you come in and see her," the nurse replied. "However, I will ask that you not spend more than five minutes in the room with Karen, as the most important thing for her to do right now is to rest."

"Got it," Leanne said, nodding. "Thank you so much."

The nurse nodded and made her way back down towards reception while Leanne and I opened the door and stepped into the room. As soon as she saw us, Karen's face broke into a huge smile. She looked almost nothing like the half-dead creature I had held in the middle of the road. Her brown hair, rather than being plastered across her face, now draped gracefully over her shoulders. Her face, which had been pale and bloodless when I saw her last, was now warm and inviting, her cheeks red. She had dimples when she smiled, and her eyes twinkled as she took us in.

"Leanne and Eliza," she said. "You're the two women who saved me. I'm so glad you came, I cannot begin to thank you enough."

"These are for you," Leanne said, handing her the flowers. "I wanted to come and apologize for, you know, hitting you. I swear, I tried to swerve. I did my best."

"You're too kind," Karen replied, reaching over to take the bouquet and inhaling deeply into the flowers. "Please, do not worry about me one bit. It's thanks to the two of you that I'm alive at all. So you must be Leanne."

My cousin nodded. "That's right, I am. And this is Eliza."

"Do you remember us hitting you?" I asked, and Karen shook her head.

"I'm afraid not. I only know what the police have told me. They said I was stabbed, and that I ran out into the road in front of you, and you're the ones who called the ambulance. I don't remember anything that happened after school ended that day. I remember the bell going off, and then waking up in the hospital bed. Everything else is a blank."

"Do you know if the police know who did this to you?"

Karen shook her head. "I don't think they do. Chief Jones himself came down to Seattle, asking me all sorts of questions. Had I been fighting with anyone, did I know anyone who might want to hurt me, that sort of thing."

"Do you?" Leanne asked. "We were just wondering ourselves who might have done it."

Karen shook her head. "Frankly, no. I've had a few disagreements with people in my life, but nothing worth killing over. I'm quite sure of that."

"What about Andrew, who runs the recreation center?" I asked. "We heard you had an argument with him a few days before you were stabbed."

Karen frowned slightly. "Now, I wonder who's been running their mouth in town. Yes, Andrew and I had a disagreement. It was very much a private matter, however, and I'm sure it wasn't something he would have killed me over. You know, I still can't even believe this is a conversation I'm having. I just can't think of anything I've ever done that would make someone want to kill me. I just can't believe it."

She was getting a little bit worked up, and obviously wasn't going to help us all that much, so I decided to try and make her feel a bit better, instead.

"It must be nice to have this community support, at least. I work with Leanne at the coffee shop and everyone I've spoken to was hoping you would pull through."

"Oh, that's just wonderful," Karen said with an appreciative smile. "I really can't believe the outpouring of support I've received from everyone here on Enchanted Enclave. Sasha came over to see me, and she made enough food to feed Kyle, the boys and my parents for weeks. A few of my coworkers came by as well and offered to take the boys out for a while so the adults could get some rest. I just can't thank everyone enough. And now these lovely flowers, when *I* should be the one thanking *you,* not the other way around."

"We'll let you rest now," I said. "Thanks for seeing us."

"Oh, thank you for coming. It's so nice to see some friendly faces from home. I'm really glad to be back here, even if it is just in the hospital."

"We were just talking about that today with Gary's sister, the florist," Leanne said.

"Janet is lovely, isn't she? She works so hard to keep

that florist going while working part time at the school. Honestly, I don't know how she does it."

"A lot of people have been saying that about you, too," I said. "After all, you've got the two little boys at home, and we know how most of the childcare falls onto the woman's shoulders."

Karen gave us a smile. "Ah, yes. Well, Kyle does do his bit sometimes. I always wish he did more, but then, what mother doesn't? The boys are really wonderful, though. My parents say they've been taking this like champions, which is what I'd expect all the way. They're so young to have their mother being hurt like this, so I try to put on the bravest face I can when they're here. They're too young to know what suffering is, and I don't want them to know about it yet, either."

"Yeah," Leanne said, nodding. "I agree. I'm really glad for their sake as well as yours that you're going to be alright."

"Me too," Karen said. "I love them so much."

We spoke for a few more minutes and then left the hospital. I was really glad Karen was alright, and it was nice to meet her when she wasn't just about to die of blood loss, but I had hoped she would have been able to give us a bit more of an indication as to who her killer was.

"Do you believe what she says about Andrew and the argument not being important?" Leanne asked, obviously thinking the same way I was.

"No," I replied. "If it hadn't been important, he wouldn't have broken into her home."

"Exactly," Leanne replied, nodding. "I agree completely. There's something there, we just have to find out what."

The problem was, I was completely out of ideas, and it seemed Leanne was as well.

*

The next morning at the coffee shop, Karen's return to town was the talk of everyone who came in to get a coffee.

"I missed you at yoga last night," Janice said to us when she came in first thing.

"Sorry," Leanne replied. "We got distracted by other things. I promise we'll be back on Wednesday."

"Speak for yourself," I muttered under my breath, and Janice gave me a knowing smile.

"It is difficult to start the practice," she told me. "However, I ask that you give it a little bit of time. No one is an expert straight away, and after you've gone to a few classes and your body has adapted to the movements you may find you feel differently."

Wow. She had to have the hearing of a bat.

"I'll be there on Wednesday," I said, the people-pleasing part of me taking over while inside my brain began sobbing at the thought.

"Good," Janice said. "I promise, it won't feel as bad the second time."

"It better not, or I might actually die right there in the yoga studio," I said after Janice left, and Leanne laughed.

"You're so dramatic. You did not almost die."

"You don't know what I felt. People have been known to die from exercising. It's happened."

"I'm pretty sure those people did more than a single hour of yoga," Leanne replied, rolling her eyes.

"You don't know that," I said, just as another customer walked in through the door, interrupting our discussion. It was Jack, looking chipper.

"Good morning," I said to him, and he smiled back at me.

"Morning. Some good news today. Karen is back at the hospital. I went and saw her late last night and I'm thrilled to report she's looking in good spirits and is on the mend."

"Yes, isn't that great?" I replied. "We went and saw her as well. She was so gracious. I'm glad she's pulled through."

"You couldn't be more right. I met her parents at the hospital. They're quite nice people, although understandably stressed. But did you hear someone broke into the family home while they were gone?"

"No!" I said, my mouth dropping open, doing my best to feign surprise. "You're kidding."

"Unfortunately not," Jack said, his mouth a grim

line. "I had no idea when I saw Karen, but I heard about it later; my wife found out about it at the bakery and told me that night."

"Is anything missing?" Leanne asked.

"That's the funny thing. Apparently, their place was ransacked a little bit, but no, nothing was gone. And there was cash and jewelry not well hidden from what I've heard. That's the worrying thing – my bet is whoever tried to kill Karen snuck into her house to try and find some incriminating evidence and get rid of it."

"Well, by all accounts it wasn't Gary," I replied.

"I heard he was in Seattle at a conference when it happened," Jack replied, frowning. "I guess that means it wasn't him after all."

"It certainly looks that way," Leanne said. "He's dropped to the bottom of our list of suspects. On the other hand, we know that Karen and Andrew had an argument about something. She won't tell us about what, and says that it wasn't important enough for him to kill her over, but we don't have any answers on that front."

"Well, hopefully the police will figure it out," Jack replied.

"Agreed," I said, handing Jack his muffin. He said goodbye to the two of us and headed off. Frankly, it didn't look like we were going to solve this crime anytime soon, so hopefully the police would manage it sooner rather than later.

CHAPTER 19

"*A*lright, time for you to take over the coffee making for a little bit," Leanne said, motioning for me to make my way to the machine. We can swap if we get a crowd, but you need to get a bit more experience."

"Sure," I said, swallowing hard and trying to hide my nerves. I was still worried that I was going to completely mess things up for customers and that they were going to hate coming to the coffee shop, but at least I had already done this once without messing things up too badly.

Our next customer was a young woman who I had seen a few times, but whose name I didn't know yet. She ordered a twelve ounce latte to go. Perfect – that was the easiest thing to make. I took a deep breath and made the coffee, carefully tamping the beans and watching as the machine extracted the espresso, the creamy brown fluid exuding that wonderful aroma that made me involuntarily inhale deeply.

Carefully steaming the milk, I added it to the coffee and handed it to the woman. "If this isn't up to our normal standard, please come back and Leanne will remake this for you," I said to her. "This is only the third coffee I've ever made, so I won't be insulted if you tell me it's terrible."

The woman laughed. "Thanks, but I'm sure it's fine. I've never had a bad coffee from here yet, and besides, as long as it's got caffeine in it, I'll drink basically anything."

"Finally, someone with low enough standards I might be able to meet them," I said with a smile, and the woman gave me a friendly smile as she took a sip.

"I don't know what you're worried about. This tastes fine. You're doing great. Thanks again, have a great day."

"You too, thank you," I said, my heart swelling happily as I realized I had just served my first ever paying customer. And she hadn't asked for a refund! Maybe I was eventually going to be good at this barista gig after all.

"Nice," Leanne said to me with an approving nod. "Good job."

I smiled, but suddenly there came a noise from above me. I looked up just in time to see one of the huge industrial-style lamps hanging from the ceiling plummeting towards me.

It took my brain a split-second to realize what was going on, and I managed to leap out of the way with a yelp just as the lamp went crashing to the ground a moment later, the sound reverberating across the room. The force of my jump knocked me off my feet and I fell against Leanne, dragging us both to the floor. A small piece of shrapnel scraped against my leg as pain seared through it.

"What in the name of Saturn?" Leanne muttered hazily as I blinked, trying to make sense of what had just happened.

"Are you alright?" a customer asked, peering over the counter as Kaillie rushed out from the kitchen.

"Leanne! Eliza! What happened?"

Aunt Debbie had been speaking with Uncle Bob on the distribution side of the building, but had rushed over at the sound, along with her brother.

Uncle Bob immediately made his way around the counter and reached down towards his daughter.

"Are you alright?" he asked us.

Still slightly dazed, I sat up a little bit and looked at what had happened. One of the lights had come crashing down from the ceiling and was now in the middle of the floor, practically unrecognizable, right where I had been standing a minute earlier. If I hadn't moved out of the way, I would have been crushed.

Someone was helping me to my feet, and I got up, unable to tear my eyes from my near-death experience. That had been one heck of an accident.

"How did that thing fall?" I heard Leanne ask next to me. "It could have killed us."

"They were only installed last year," Kaillie said, frowning. "And we got Yuri, the best contractor in town to install them. He wouldn't have done a shoddy job."

Uncle Bob stepped past me to have a look at the wire that had led from the lamp to the ceiling. His face was grim as he held it up.

"I don't think this was an accident," he said quietly, and I gasped.

"Someone cut it on purpose?" Leanne asked, and Uncle Bob nodded.

"Yes. About ninety percent of the cable was sliced through cleanly, cut with a knife or some other sort of blade. Only about ten percent is actually torn. I think someone came in here and cut through most of the cable, expecting the rest of it to eventually tear off and crash to the ground."

I looked over at Leanne, who shared my horrified look.

"But... who would do something like that?" I asked. "When?"

Uncle Bob shook his head. "I don't know. If the two of you are alright to move, I think we need to clear away from this area and call the police."

A sinking feeling developed in the pit of my stomach. Someone had tampered with the lamp on purpose?

Aunt Debbie took over quickly and motioned for the customers to head back to the tables. I could hear her reassuring them, telling them that they were in no danger, but that if any of them wanted to take their items to go that wasn't a problem.

Most of them were trying to look past Aunt Debbie and looked over at Leanne and me, so I flashed a reassuring smile as best I could while Kaillie took Leanne and I to the kitchen at the back.

"What on earth happened?" she asked, and I shook my head.

"I have no idea. I just heard a snap, then I looked up and the lamp was falling. I just got out of the way instinctively."

"It's a good thing you did," Leanne replied. "If you were still under there when it hit the ground you'd be dead for sure. Those lamps are *heavy.*"

"And Uncle Bob said someone did it on purpose. That means someone just tried to kill you, Eliza."

My face paled at the idea. It wasn't the first time my life had been in danger since moving here, and in fact a killer had tried to silence me before, but this was different. That time, I'd had a gun leveled right at me when I had confronted the killer. This time, I was just going about my day-to-day life and almost had it ended in the blink of an eye. Just like that.

Who on earth would have done this to me?

"You realize it was probably whoever tried to kill Karen, right?" Kaillie said softly.

"How could they have gotten in? When did they do it? This might actually be a good thing. If we can solve this crime, that can confirm for us who tried to kill Karen. If it was Andrew, maybe he left his fingerprints on the lamp or something like that," Leanne said. "It sucks, but it might get us a bit closer to solving Karen's stabbing."

I wasn't quite in a mental state to be looking at the positives to this event yet. Kaillie must have noticed, because she made her way towards me.

"Hey, come on over here and sit down," she said, motioning to a small bench in the corner that she must have used to take breaks. "Leanne, can you get Eliza some water or something? She's not looking so hot."

"Are you hurt?" Leanne asked, grabbing a water bottle from the fridge and bringing it over to me.

"No," I said, shaking my head. "I mean, I think I have a cut on my leg, but it's not too bad. It hurt at first, but it's fine now. I'm just a bit shaken up."

"That's understandable," Leanne said, leaning down to look at my leg. "After all, someone just tried to kill you. But listen, if anything, this just makes me more determined to find out who did this."

I winced as Leanne moved her finger towards the cut. "Kaillie, you have a first aid kit back here, right?"

"Yeah," my cousin replied, making her way towards one of the shelves near the door. She grabbed a sealed tub and brought it over to us. Leanne quickly took care of the cut, cleaning the wound, putting s magical potion to heal the cut immediately, and then covering it with a large bandage.

"Thanks," I said with a smile when she was finished. "I appreciate that."

"You're lucky you got away with just that scratch," Leanne said, shaking her head. "I can't believe it. It also means someone broke into the coffee shop. And they had to have done it in secret, or else we would have noticed. It's not like the window in the door was broken this morning or anything like that."

"Right," I said. "You didn't notice anything strange when you unlocked it this morning?"

"No," Leanne replied. "On the other hand, I can't guarantee that I would have noticed anything out of the ordinary at all. I've unlocked that front door in the morning probably over a thousand times in my life. I tend to do it on autopilot now. If the door had been unlocked and I just turned the key around an already unbolted door I might not even have noticed, to be completely honest."

"That makes things harder," I said with a frown. "What about back doors?"

"There's one here," Kaillie said, motioning to a door on the side wall. "This one leads to the alley at the side, which makes it easy for me to take out the trash when I'm baking. But there's no way to unlock it from the outside, and I'm one hundred percent sure it was locked from the inside when I got here this morning."

"The other option is from dad's side in the warehouse," Leanne mused. "There are a few entrances there, including the rolling door that leads to the loading dock at the back. Whoever did it probably came through there."

"Do you know if Andrew has any particular lock-picking skills?" I asked, and Leanne shook her head.

"I'm afraid I don't have a clue. I never heard about it. If that sort of information ever got out he'd probably lose his job as the manager at the recreation center. After all, you can't have someone with a criminal record working around so many kids like that."

"Good point," I conceded. "I'm guessing this place doesn't have security cameras?"

Kaillie gave me a sad smile. "Unfortunately, no. Heck, we don't even have an alarm system. It's not like we have a sky-high crime rate here on Enchanted Enclave. And while the coffee here might be delicious, it's about the only thing on the premises that would be worth stealing after hours that you could do without being noticed. The coffee machine would take a while to unhook, and the roasters in the back are worth a lot of money but also weigh a ton. Literally."

"And up until now we never considered that someone might break in and try to kill one of us," Leanne added quietly.

The three of us sat in silence, absorbing those words, until a minute later the door to the kitchen opened and in walked Detective Ross Andrews.

CHAPTER 20

"Hello, ladies," he said in greeting, nodding to each one of us in turn. "I'm wondering if I could speak with the three of you about today's events."

We nodded, and his eyes immediately fell on the first aid kit, and my left pants leg which was rolled up to my knee, exposing the bandage.

"Are you alright?" he asked, concern written all over his face.

"I'm fine, thanks. It's just a scratch." The intensity of his stare made my face redden slightly, and I found myself wishing that he would reach down and touch my leg. What on earth was wrong with me? Just because he was good-looking didn't mean I had to practically slobber all over him.

"Are you sure? I can take you to the hospital if you'd like. They can give you stitches if you need it."

I shook my head. "Thanks, but seriously, it's fine.

Just a scratch, that's all. It could have been a lot worse though."

"I saw," he replied, his expression grim.

"So your being here confirms it – Dad was right and someone did slice the wire on the ramp, rigging it to fall on Eliza."

Detective Andrews nodded. "That's right. When I first heard about what had happened I hoped it was a hoax. After all, surely nobody would do anything like that here in Enchanted Enclave. But I had a look for myself, and there's no way it was anything else. Which one of you unlocked the front door this morning?"

"I did," Leanne said. "Eliza and I got here about five minutes before Aunt Debbie, and I was the one with the key of the two of us."

"Did you notice anything out of the ordinary?"

"No, but I was saying to the others before, I'm not sure I would have noticed even if there was something. I basically open up the front door on autopilot. Still, I'd look at the back entrances. The door between the warehouse side of things and the coffee shop is never locked, even at night, so whoever did it may have come in through there."

"How did they get up to the wire?" I asked. "After all, it was pretty high up. He would have needed a ladder to get up there."

"There is one in the warehouse side of the building, which lends credence to Leanne's theory that he may have come in through an entrance on that side. I'll go over there next. Can you think of anyone who might have wanted to kill you?"

I squirmed in my seat. After all, the answer was yes: whoever had stabbed Karen. But admitting that to Detective Andrews would mean admitting that I had been investigating the attack on Karen, and I had a sneaking suspicion he wasn't going to be a big fan of that if I told him.

Still, I came inches away from being crushed to death by an industrial lamp today. As much as a part of me wanted Detective Andrews to be pleased with me – and I pushed away the feeling that it was more than just the same normal desire I always had for everyone to like me – I figured he'd probably be less pleased if the person who had tried to first kill Karen and then kill me eventually succeeded.

"It might be Andrew Lloyd, who I'm pretty sure stabbed Karen," I replied. Kaillie looked horrified, like someone had just told the principal she deserved to get detention, while Leanne just nodded grimly, obviously agreeing with my assessment that Detective Andrews should know what we had been doing.

If he was angry, his reaction didn't betray it. In fact, the only reaction he had at all was raising a single eyebrow. "And why do you think the person who stabbed Karen may have tried to kill you, too?"

"Well, the thing is, we may have been asking a few questions here and there," I offered, trying to sound as casual as possible. "After all, working in the coffee shop you get to know a lot of people, and right now everyone is asking about the murder. So it's come up a lot in conversation."

"Right, I'm sure that's all it is. Someone wants to kill you because you contributed to the local rumor mill in your coffee shop."

"Ok, so we may also have gone and had a chat with a few people who may have had a reason to want Karen dead," I admitted. "It's possible that one of the people we spoke to – who almost certainly tried to kill Karen – decided we were on the right track and wanted to take care of the problem."

I tried not to think too hard about the fact that *I* was the problem in question.

"And now we're getting to the crux of it," Detective Andrews said. "You seriously shouldn't be going around investigating this. I'm telling you, as a police officer, I can do my job."

"We know you can, but it's not like Chief Jones is the sharpest tool in the shed," Leanne argued. "And he's still in charge overall. Besides, four heads are better than one, right?"

"Not when only one of those heads has actual law enforcement experience, and the other ones are now potentially becoming the wannabe killer's next targets," Detective Andrews pointed out. "Look, I actually understand why the three of you have been looking into this, but you can't keep doing it. It's too dangerous, and one of you is going to get hurt." He looked pointedly at me. "Or worse."

"Message received," Kaillie said, nodding. "Don't worry, we want to be good. We'll do the right thing."

"Speak for yourself," I heard Leanne mutter under her breath, but when Detective Andrews looked over at her she just flashed him a million-watt smile.

"Alright, well, tell me who it is you spoke to," Detective Andrews said.

"Kaillie spoke to Andrew, from the recreation center," Leanne said. "He's our number one suspect right now."

"Is he, now?" Detective Andrews asked.

"Yes," I replied firmly. "He was seen arguing with Karen not long before she was stabbed. She won't tell us what they were arguing about, but it was definitely something. Plus, he got super defensive when Kaillie started talking to him."

"Perhaps it was because you accused him of stabbing a woman. Most people don't take too kindly to that, especially when it's just a member of the public doing it. After all, you're not cops."

"It was more than that," Kaillie said slowly. "He barely even allowed us to get to the accusatory part. As soon as we started talking about Karen all of his defenses went up, and he wouldn't say anything else, just told us to get away from him."

"Alright," Detective Andrews said. "Who else have you spoken to?"

"Gary Vanderchuck," Leanne replied. "That's it."

She wisely didn't mention Kyle, and I was glad for it. After all, his place had been broken into, and I was there when Detective Andrews had gotten the phone call about it, and if Detective Andrews knew we were considering Kyle as a suspect he might also start to wonder if we were the ones who had broken into his place.

"Why don't you think he did it?"

"He has an alibi," I replied without skipping a beat. "He was at a conference in Seattle when Karen was stabbed."

Detective Andrews raised his eyebrows. "You certainly have been busy. I'll give you credit for thoroughness." Still, I couldn't help but feel like there was something in his look that I was missing, like he knew something I didn't. He probably wouldn't be thrilled if I grabbed his notebook and started flipping through it.

I figured we could do without admitting we were looking inside the owners' cars to check for blood, as well. Detective Andrews had probably done that himself, among other things.

"Alright, well, who do you think did it?" I asked. "Surely at this point you've got a prime suspect. Do you think we're on the right track, or do you think we're way off base?"

Detective Andrews smiled at me, and butterflies fluttered in my stomach. "You can't honestly think I'm going to tell you that, can you? That's confidential. I can confirm that I have a number of persons of interest who are being considered as likely culprits in the attack on Karen. But what about anyone else? Can you think of others who might want to hurt you?"

I shook my head. "No. The most dangerous thing I've done apart from looking into the attack on Karen is a yoga class last week. And the only person who wanted to kill me after that ended was myself."

I got a laugh from Detective Andrews for that little quip. "Alright, so no disagreements with anyone else?"

"Definitely not. Not even by a customer at the coffee shop who short-changed me. I'm telling you, there's only one person who could have wanted me dead: the person who tried to kill Karen."

"Got it," Detective Andrews said, and turned to Leanne. "What about you? After all, the both of you work behind that counter together. It's possible the killer was going after you instead."

"Sorry, I'm my usual charming self at all times, and no one wants to kill me. Well, apart from Eliza for dragging her to the yoga class in question, but I can say with confidence she didn't do it."

"Because it could have maimed her as well?"

"Oh please, if the lamp had killed me at least I'd never have to step foot in that studio again," I muttered in reply.

"Because Eliza stomps around like an elephant at home and I would have heard her going out," Leanne said with a grin, and I stuck my tongue out at her quickly. Detective Andrews laughed.

"Alright. I think the two of you are right then, if there was no one else you've had any disagreements with this probably has to do with the attempt on Karen's life."

"Do you know who broke into her house the other day?" I blurted out before I convinced myself it was a bad idea. "We heard someone did."

"Right. And where exactly did you hear that?"

"You know, just town gossip," I replied. "Does that mean it really happened, then?"

"Yes, it happened. And no, I'm not telling you anything about it."

I frowned, but I really couldn't have expected any other answer.

"Alright, thanks," Detective Andrews said, standing up. "I appreciate the help, and I promise you, I am going to do whatever needs to be done to find the person who did this. Someone tried to kill one of you two, and I take that very seriously. You should know I've spoken to Debbie and the coffee shop will be closed for the rest of the day while I bring in a full crime scene investigation unit to try and find more clues as to who is responsible for this."

"Thank you," I told him earnestly. As much as the police chief in town might have been an idiot, I believed Detective Andrews when he said he was working hard, and it really did put my heart a little bit more at ease knowing he was going to try and find the person who had done this.

"I'm happy to do it. It's my job, and I want to remind you that it's not your job, just like it's not your job to try and figure out who stabbed Karen. You could be dead because you stuck your nose in something you shouldn't have."

"Yeah, but we're not," Leanne countered, and Detective Andrews gave her an incredulous look.

"Only because Eliza here has decent reflexes and heard the snap of the wire. You can't count on luck any more. I don't want to see you hurt, Eliza. I don't want to see any of you hurt. Stay out of this."

Then, without another word, Detective Andrews headed back into the main part of the coffee shop.

"Did you hear that?" Leanne said to me with a grin. "He doesn't want to see you get hurt."

"Please," I scoffed. "He said that to everyone."

"Yeah, but he was looking right at you when he said it. And he singled you out. He added Kaillie and me as an afterthought."

"That's silly," I said, brushing Leanne's words aside.

"Eliza and Ross, sitting in a tree, K-I-S-S-I-N-G," Leanne teased.

"You know, that song is pretty appropriate, seeing as you're acting about twelve years old," I replied, looking to Kaillie to help me out.

"I agree with Leanne," my cousin said, and my mouth dropped open. "What? It's obvious he likes you.

There's definitely a spark between the two of you. Plus, you immediately go the shade of a tomato every time he looks at you. It's kind of a giveaway."

"I do not," I replied, my face going hot.

"Yeah, just like that," Leanne said with a laugh. "That's exactly it."

I groaned and leaned back against the wall. "You have got to be kidding me."

"Just ask him out."

"What?" I yelped. "No way. Why would I do that?"

"Because you're obviously attracted to him, and he's obviously attracted to you. That's how this whole things works. Or do you not know that?"

"No. No way. I'm not asking him out. Besides, you don't know he feels like that about me. Maybe you're just projecting. And *I* don't feel that way about him to begin with."

"Sure you don't. The fact that you added that almost as an afterthought really seals it," Kaillie said, smiling.

I grumbled at my cousins. I *totally* didn't have a thing for Detective Andrews. I mean sure, he was really nice, and whenever he smiled dimples appeared in his cheeks. And his body looked like he did yoga *constantly*. And hit the weight room a few times a week too, for good measure. But that didn't mean I liked him.

"Whatever you say," Leanne said. "You'll see. The two of you are going to end up together one day. I just know it."

She was so wrong.

CHAPTER 21

*W*ith nothing to do for the rest of the morning or the afternoon, with the coffee shop being closed, the three of us decided to stop by Otterly Delicious to get a bite to eat and hopefully come up with a new plan to find out who had tried to kill Karen... and now to figure out who had tried to kill Leanne and me, too.

We ordered the soup and sandwich combo – I was getting a BLT along with a bowl of curried cauliflower soup – and sat down in one of the booths.

"We should have stuck around and tried to get as much information as we could from the crime scene people," Leanne bemoaned.

I shook my head. "I don't think it would have worked. I noticed Detective Andrews looking at us as we were leaving; I think he was expecting us to do that.

If we had tried to ask anyone anything he probably would have stopped us and told us to head on home."

"Of course you would have noticed that," Leanne said to me with a wink.

"Oh let it go," I replied. "I'm not going out with him."

"Sure, you say that now. Anyway, I will let it go, but only because I want to catch this person. I mean, it's one thing to go after Karen. But this time *I* could have been killed, and that's even worse," Leanne said, and Kaillie snorted.

"Karen is way better a person than you."

"Yeah, that's probably true," Leanne admitted. "Still, it would suck to die, so we need to find proof that Andrew stabbed her."

"Agreed," I said. "I don't plan on dying either. "So let's find some proof, and maybe submit it anonymously to Detective Andrew so he doesn't keep thinking that we're investigating this case."

"Because you care so much about his approval?" Leanne asked with a grin, and I glared at her in reply.

"Ok," Kaillie said. "So what do we need to know?"

"I want to know who he was on the phone with," I said. "If we can get that information, maybe we'll have a new lead. But you can't exactly get away with stealing someone's phone these days. And what if he has facial recognition to unlock it?"

"That's easily taken care of with a spell, we just have

to convince Kaillie to do it," Leanne said, and the two of us looked at her expectantly.

"Fine," Kaillie said, following it up with a big huff to make sure we knew she wasn't happy about it.

"Really? That easy?" Leanne asked. "I was sure you were going to give us a lecture about how you can't use magic for bad and how you're not going to give up your shot to return to the paranormal world just for us."

"Normally, I would have. But someone tried to kill you two today. And frankly, even if it meant never visiting the paranormal world in my life, I would do whatever it took to make sure the person responsible doesn't get a chance to do it again."

"Aww, that's the sweetest thing you've ever said," Leanne replied. "Plus, now we've figured out what the line is. If we want Kaillie to use magic in a bad way, it has to be so that she can find someone trying to kill us."

"Well, let's hope you don't make that a habit," she replied. "But yes. If this is what it takes to save your life, then so be it."

"Alright, let's do that this afternoon after we eat," I said. As if right on cue, the waitress arrived with our food and the three of us spent the next quarter of an hour talking about other things while eating, getting ready for a busy afternoon ahead.

Hopefully, by the time it was over, we would have proof that Andrew had tried to kill Karen, and we'd be able to let Detective Andrews know so he could arrest him.

"Hey, speak of the devil," I said suddenly, noticing a familiar figure on the sidewalk. It was Andrew.

"Let's follow him," Leanne said, jumping up from the booth. Kaillie and I followed immediately after her.

"Stay back a bit," Kaillie warned. "He already knows we're trying to prove he stabbed Karen. And if he tried to kill you two already, well, you never know what he'll do if he sees us following him."

"He might not even be doing anything suspicious. Maybe it's his lunch break or something."

"Yeah, sure. The murderer isn't doing anything weird. Kaillie, cast an invisibility spell on us. We're going to need it."

I could see Kaillie trying to figure out how she could get away with spying on a non-magical person without casting the invisibility spell, but she must have realized pretty quickly that it was, in fact, the best way to spy on someone without them knowing.

"Fine," she hissed, motioning for us to enter a nearby alley so she could cast the spell without being seen. "Hurry."

A couple of seconds later the three of us were invisible and we made our way back into the street. He had continued about thirty feet further than when I'd last seen him, but I still spotted Andrew. He was headed in the opposite direction from the recreation center.

I rushed after him, careful to hold out my hands in

front of me so as not to crash into one of my cousins. Eventually, he reached one of the local bar and restaurant combo establishments and went inside. Thankfully, the door was a slow-closing one, and I was able to sneak in afterwards, with one of my cousins stepping on the back of my heel as she followed in closely behind.

"Sorry," I heard Leanne whisper quietly into my ear.

As soon as we were in I took a few steps to the left of the door to have a look around where it was unlikely that anyone would walk into me suddenly. This was a typical-looking Irish pub, with dark walls, dark carpet, warm lighting, and beer on tap. The menus were leather-bound, and a couple of casually-dressed waitresses made their way between tables. About a quarter of them were filled, with everyone here looking fairly casual and plates on most of the tables. After all, it was still ten to noon, so I suspected most people here at this hour were more about the eating than the drinking.

Andrew had gone straight to a booth at the back, in the far corner. I couldn't see the person he was meeting with, but I headed over there, careful to take a path that would keep me as far as possible from anyone else. I had to be as subtle as I could. I was also taking special care to make sure I didn't accidentally hit one of my cousins and send us both careening into a table. That would definitely not qualify as a subtle use of magic.

"What are you doing here? I can't meet you here, in public like this," Andrew hissed at the person across the table from him. The man looked, well, a lot like Andrew. They had the same eyes and mouth, though the man across from him had a good thirty pounds on the recreation center administrator.

"Relax," the man replied, leaning back in the booth casually. "Stop looking so suspicious. No one cares that we're here."

"I care. I can't have us meeting like this. The risks are too high."

There was a nudge next to my shoulder; one of the others was obviously listening in as well.

"You only think there are risks right now because of what happened to that woman."

"Yeah, she almost died. And people saw me arguing with her a few days before. What if she tells the police everything?"

"She won't. If she hasn't done it yet, she's not going to. Besides, you could always arrange for her to have an accident in the hospital, or something like that. There's nothing saying she has to come out of this alive."

"You're insane. After everything that's happened she's bound to have extra security around her. No, I'm not going near her with a ten-foot pole now. I don't want the two of us to be associated in any way."

"Did you get the papers from her house, then?"

"Yeah, I found them. She had scans of them on her computer. That's all the proof she had, so there's no more. And her husband's not going to say anything either, obviously. So I'm all good on that front. But I don't like this. I don't like meeting you in public, Tony."

"Why, because your dear old brother has a criminal record and you don't?"

"No, because my brother is actively involved in criminal activity."

"And so are you. But the difference is you like to pretend to be better than me, when the reality is we're exactly the same. The difference is I accept what I'm doing, whereas you just like the money."

"No, we're not the same. I do like the money, I will admit that. But I can't do it anymore. I can't keep running bets for you. I keep thinking I'm going to get caught. Karen threatened to turn me in if I didn't stop. So I'm going to stop. Do you know how long it's been since I've had a good night's sleep? I can't handle the stress. I just can't do it."

"If you stop doing this for me, I'm going to turn you in for breaking into Karen's house."

"You know what? That's fine. Because even if I have to spend time in prison, that's better than dying. And at this point, I literally feel like if I keep going this way, my heart's going to explode, Tony. You're my brother. You're supposed to be on my side on these things. I'm telling you, I just can't."

"Fine," Tony said, standing up. "From now on, consider yourself out. I won't come to you anymore, but if I hear that you've gone into business for yourself, I'm not going to be happy."

Andrew raised his hands. "Trust me, you don't have to worry about me. I'm out of this business for good. I'm going back to my job. The extra money is in my bank account, and that's where it's going to stay. I'll live with my salary."

"You better. And the next time you find yourself in trouble, don't come to me if you're not prepared to play the game."

"Sure thing, Tony. No problem. I'll leave you alone. I learned my lesson."

"Good. I did you a favor, and you're backing out on it. And I get it. Really, I do. This lifestyle isn't for everyone. But I can't do this for you again."

"Got it. Thanks, Tony. I appreciate you letting me get out of this without breaking my kneecaps." Andrew laughed nervously, and Tony grinned at him.

"There's that sense of humor. You know, it's too bad we drifted apart so much. We were actually good buds, and I gotta say, I enjoyed working with you. You brought in a decent amount of money considering the tiny population that lives on this miserable island. I'm telling you, take your earnings and come move to the city. It's much more fun."

Andrew shook his head. "Nah. Thanks, but I like it here. The slower pace is way more my speed. I should have known I didn't belong in your world. I'm better off behind my desk at the recreation center, organizing classes for kids and shooting hoops with them when I've got a spare minute."

He got up from the table, and already looked visibly more relaxed. There was still some obvious tension in his shoulders, but some of the lines on his face seemed to have disappeared instantly.

"Take care of yourself, bro," Tony called out. "I'm telling you, you don't need to do anything stupid."

"Yeah. You're right, I don't."

I only wondered if Andrew already *had* done something stupid. After all, he had never once in that meeting admitted that he didn't stab Karen.

CHAPTER 22

*A*ndrew left the bar and started actually whistling as he walked back down the street towards the recreation center. I looked around for my cousins, but it was fruitless. They were invisible in the same way as I was. But I needed Kaillie to be able to undo the invisibility spell so that we could confront Andrew.

"Kaillie?" I said quietly, hoping she was within about ten feet of me and would be able to hear what I said, but no, nothing. I had no choice but to follow Andrew on my own and hope that I'd run into one of my cousins – quite literally – sooner rather than later.

Of course, I did have the option of reversing the spell myself. I fingered my wand in my pocket, where I always kept it. I had seen Kaillie cast the spell multiple times, and I was fairly certain I knew the words to it off by heart. But still, what if something went wrong?

What if I messed it up? Tina had told me it was completely acceptable to take my time, and to wait until I was comfortable doing things. If I messed up reversing this spell, I could ruin my entire life. What if I paralyzed myself by accident? I'd have no way of letting anyone know what had happened.

I knew I was eventually going to have to use magic in public, and use spells that had a little bit of inherent risk. But I was a beginner, and I really didn't want to try it out just yet. Tina had told me that was fine, and I was going to go with her advice after all.

"Eliza" a small voice to my right suddenly asked. It was Leanne.

"Hey," I replied quietly. "Where's Kaillie?"

"Over here," my other cousin said. "Come on, let's go behind this building and reverse the spell. I think it's safe to say Andrew is going to the recreation center."

"Right," I said, and the three of us walked behind the store in question, where Kaillie quickly made the three of us visible once more. I looked at my arms and hands in awe, still not used to the idea of being able to use magic to become invisible, but impressed by it all the same.

"I think we should go confront him," Leanne said.

"You always think that," I retorted.

"That's because it's always the right answer."

"It's definitely not always the right answer," Kaillie said. "But in this case, I think you might be right. Andrew sounded like a man who's desperate. If we tell him we know he was taking illegal bets for residents but promise not to tell anyone if he tells us everything, he might actually spill the beans."

"See?" Leanne said, nodding. "Perfect plan."

"Well, I don't have a better idea, so let's go for it," I replied.

Five minutes later we were at the recreation center, and Leanne knocked on the door leading to Andrew's office, near the concession stand.

"Come in," he said, and as I opened the door there was a smile on his face, but when he saw my cousins it turned to a scowl. "What, are you here to accuse me of murder again?"

"Yes, only this time we've got more evidence," Leanne said, stepping forward. "We know you've been taking bets illegally in this town. We know Kyle was one of your customers, and that's why Karen threatened to turn you in. That's why you stabbed her, isn't it?"

Andrew's face went a deep shade of red, and then almost as quickly, completely white. He started off looking like he was going to stand up from his chair and start pummeling Leanne, but then he changed his mind and sighed, sinking deeper into it, an obviously broken man.

"I didn't stab Karen. I swear to you, I didn't. I will admit to the rest. But please, don't tell anyone. I'm not in that game anymore. I've gotten out. I never meant to do it, and I never meant to break the law. But I'm telling you, I didn't stab Karen."

"Why don't you tell us the whole story?" I suggested kindly. After all, we still only had bits and pieces of it, and Leanne had basically guessed the connection between Andrew and Kyle. I wanted all of it, and it sounded like Andrew was finally ready to give it all up.

Andrew nodded.

"Alright. I will, because I want you to know I'm not a bad person. I didn't stab Karen. About a year ago, I had some financial trouble. Basically, my car blew up at the same time as my fridge, and I couldn't pay for both. Because of some stupid mistakes I made when I was younger, I couldn't get a credit card – my credit is completely trashed – but I live on the east side of the island. I also didn't want to walk half an hour to work and back every day, and I also needed food. I needed some extra cash, so I went to my brother, Tony. He always told me growing up that if I ever needed anything, I should come to him. And I believed him. After all, Tony's my big brother. So I go to see him, and I ask him for a bit of cash. And he tells me he'll give it to me, but I have to work for it."

"What does Tony do, exactly?" Kaillie asked. "He's a criminal, but what kind?"

"I don't know," Andrew said, shaking his head. "You're right that he's a criminal, but I honestly try and stay out of that side of his life as much as possible. I don't know if he's hooked up with a gang, or the mafia, or if he works on his own, or what. But he told me he was running book, and he wanted to expand his services, and thought that Enchanted Enclave would be perfect. Plus, he told me I had the perfect job for it. Everyone comes to the recreation center at times. Maybe it's just a guy dropping his kids off to play hockey, or someone stopping at the gym for a workout after a big day at the office. Either way, Tony said, they'd be able to make a quick pit stop to my office, place a bet or two, and then head on home. It would be super easy money. And he was right."

Andrew sighed, as if collecting his thoughts for a second, and then continued. "He was so right. Word got around the island, and before I knew it, I was collecting hundreds, thousands of dollars a night in betting money. I would take the ferry over to the mainland and give it back to my brother. My cut alone was more than my entire salary. Within a week I'd bought a new car and fridge. But honestly, it never sat right with me. After that, every cent I earned I stuck in a savings account, and I refused to touch it. I didn't like how I earned the money. I didn't like sneaking around. I didn't like how my chest would seize up every time I spotted a law enforcement official. Chief Ron came into the recreation center one day and I almost had a heart attack. It turned out he was just looking for a teenager whose parents didn't know where he was, but it scared the crap out of me. I'd never seen Chief Ron anywhere near the recreation center before."

"So how did Karen come into play?" I asked. "When did she get involved?"

"When she confronted her husband about his gambling and he admitted to her that I was the one who had been taking the bets for him. That was what the argument between us was about. I was trying to get her to keep her mouth shut; I didn't want her to tell the cops anything. And she wanted me to stop taking bets. She told me it was wrong, and that it was ruining this community. And you know what? She was right. We definitely fought, I'm not going to deny that. But it was my ego doing the fighting. After I'd had a few hours to settle down I realized she was right, and I called her that night. I told her that I'd come to my senses, and that I was going to tell my brother that I wasn't doing it anymore. She thanked me, and told me that it was the right thing to do. You know, Karen was right about that. You have no idea the stress this was putting me under. I didn't enjoy it."

"And that was the conversation you had with your brother today."

"That's right. This was the third time, in fact. I called him a couple of other times, but he pushed back a lot harder. I guess he finally realized I was serious about it. Karen was stabbed a couple days after I spoke to her on the phone. The first time, Tony tried to convince me that it was a good thing, that this way I could keep working for him. But I guess he realized I'm serious after all."

"Hold on," Kaillie said. "Do you think *Tony* could have stabbed Karen?"

Andrew shook his head. "No, he couldn't have. I mean, if he knew who she was, sure. I actually wouldn't have put it past him. But I never told him who the person I was arguing with was. He didn't have a name, so it would have been impossible for him to find her."

"You're *sure* you didn't let her name slip at all?"

"One hundred percent," Andrew said. I barely mentioned her at all. I wanted Tony to think that it was my own decision, and that it wasn't really influenced by anyone else."

"How can we know for sure you didn't stab Karen?"

"You can't," Andrew said with a shrug. "I was in my office until after nine, and there aren't any security cameras in here. There are a few in the building, but there are also a dozen ways to get in and out of this place while avoiding them. But I'm telling you, I didn't do it."

"You're the one who broke into her house though, aren't you?" I asked. I figured if he was willing to admit to that, then maybe he was telling the truth about not having stabbed her.

"Yes, that was me. Karen mentioned that her husband had kept a record of everything he bet, in case I tried to rip him off. When I found out she was stabbed, I figured the police would eventually search her place looking for clues, and I had to get rid of those papers before they did. It took me a couple of days before I was able to build up the nerve to actually go in there and get them, but I did. They were on the laptop. I had to really psyche myself up to do it. I'm not like Tony. I'm not a criminal through-and-through, and I didn't know what I was doing. I was scared as anything as I left, and I was sure I was going to get caught, but I didn't. Not until you three came along, anyway. Are you going to tell the cops on me?"

He looked up at us now, a completely broken man.

"I don't know," Leanne said. "You say you're never going to do anything like this again?"

"Never," Andrew said, shaking his head. "Absolutely never. You have my word."

"We'll have to discuss it, but I think maybe we don't need to let the police know, either. Unless we find out you stabbed Karen. In which case, we're telling them everything."

"Of course. But I'm telling you, I really didn't. I had nothing against Karen. She was just looking out for her family, and I respect that. I didn't stab her."

"Ok," I said, nodding. "Let's say we believe you. Who do you think did it?"

A pained expression crossed Andrew's face. "I have no idea. I'm telling you, I barely knew her. Her boys took soccer lessons here, so I knew her to say hi to, but that was it. We weren't close, and I have no idea as to who would want her dead."

I was tempted to believe him. Honestly, Andrew had sounded like he was giving us straight answers from the start. Looking at Leanne and Kaillie, I had a sneaking suspicion they thought the same as we did.

"Alright," Kaillie said finally. "We make no promises about what we're going to do with the information, but we appreciate you being straight with us."

"Seriously, if there was anything – anything at all I could do to prove that I hadn't stabbed Karen, I would do it. I'm telling you, it wasn't me."

The three of us headed out of the office and back into the street.

CHAPTER 23

"What do you think?" Leanne asked as soon as we burst out of the recreation center and back into the daylight. "Was he being straight with us?"

"I think so," Kaillie replied. "Everything he said to us matched up with what we overheard in the conversation with his brother, and he had no way of knowing we were listening in on that."

"I agree," I said. "Plus, he even admitted that he broke into Karen's home. He seems to me like a guy who got in way over his head, did some bad things, and wants to have to pay for them. You know how some killers end up having the guilt gnaw away at them so badly they turn themselves in? That was the impression I got from Andrew. And despite all of that, he still didn't admit that he'd stabbed Karen. I think more than anything, that's what makes me believe him."

"Alright, so he's not our killer after all. Who does that leave us with?"

"Kyle," Kaillie said. "Since Gary was apparently at that conference. He didn't have the opportunity to do it."

"It's always the husband," Leanne replied. "He must have found out that Karen was going to divorce him, and decided that he'd rather she be dead. We can go in and see him later. Eliza and I are going to yoga class."

I groaned. "I was *really* hoping you'd forgotten about that."

Leanne pouted at me. "You said you were going to give it another shot."

"No, *you* said that I should give it another shot. There's a big difference."

"Come on," Leanne whined. "I promise it's not going to be as bad as last time. And besides, I'm not going to stop pestering you, ever, so you might as well get it over with."

I sighed. "Fine. I guess I'll go. But if I die there tonight, let it be known that I didn't want to."

"Don't worry, I'll spread the word that you were murdered by a yoga practice," Kaillie said.

"Thank you. Alright, let's head home and grab a change of clothes, then we can go."

Twenty minutes later I was standing in front of Janice's yoga studio on Main Street, looking at the door, willing the ground to open up and swallow me.

"Come on, stop being a baby and come inside,"

Leanne said, opening the door and motioning for me to follow. I supposed the longer I put this off, the more painful it was going to be, so I sighed and followed her in.

I dawdled as much as I could in the change room, with Leanne glaring at me the whole time. "I know what you're doing. You're acting like a child. No one is fooled by you."

"If we're late, then that's one less minute of yoga I need to do today."

"If we're late I'm going to make you come another time to make up for it," Leanne replied, and I scowled.

"Oh come on, that's not fair."

"Hey, if you're going to act like a child, I'm going to treat you like one. Yoga is good for you. You look like you haven't exercised in years. Your arms are as toned as a pool noodle."

"I happen to like my pool noodle arms, thank you very much." Still, as much as I liked to complain to Leanne about how much the last yoga class I had taken felt like death, I knew she was right. I had nothing remotely resembling muscle tone, and my exercise regimen could kindly be described as "inspired by a Sloth". So if it meant actually being vaguely in shape for the first time in my life maybe I could struggle through a second class, in the hopes that it wouldn't hurt as much as the first class.

Besides, yoga had the advantage of being done

indoors. I had a sneaking suspicion that in the winter I'd consider that a huge advantage.

I trudged towards the studio, grabbed one of the mats available for those who didn't have their own, and set myself up among all the strong, lithe people in the room and prepared for another hour of torture that I was going to have to pay for.

An hour later I had collapsed back onto my mat, but while I felt like I wasn't going to be able to move for the next day, that was a significant improvement over the previous class, when I strongly contemplated throwing myself out the window, except that I didn't have the strength.

"So what's the verdict?" Leanne asked, standing over me. I groaned and sat up. "You're moving on your own this time, so that's an improvement."

"I guess it was a little bit easier."

"See?" Janice said, coming over with a knowing smile. "The practice of yoga can be difficult for beginners, but once you get used to the movements, your body gets used to the exercise and the poses, and you will begin to feel more in tune with your body. I do hope you'll continue to join us in future sessions. Namaste."

"See?" Leanne said as she led me back to the change rooms. "It wasn't that bad. Besides, yoga opens your mind and your body. Don't you feel more relaxed, and like your brain has just taken a break?"

"That's because it's taken off and run down the road

as fast as it possibly can to get away from this body," I replied. Deep down, however, I had to admit that Leanne was right. I felt refreshed, energized, and limber, like one of those inflatable men in front of car dealerships.

Maybe there really *was* something to this whole yoga thing.

"Fine, I admit it, maybe this isn't as bad as I made it out to be last time. But I still reserve the right to complain."

"Works for me," Leanne said, laughing. "I'm thinking of starting a new Twitter account that just records the things you complain about when you come to yoga. I'll probably be a celebrity within a few months."

"Sure," I said, laughing. Suddenly, I paused.

"What is it?" Leanne asked.

I looked at her and grinned. "I know who stabbed Karen and tried to kill us."

"What? That came to you, just now?"

"Hey, you're the one who said yoga clears your head. Maybe that's what did it. I was finally able to think clearly for a second, and it just came to me."

"Well, who is it?"

I looked around the change room. It was totally empty. "Gary Vanderchuk, the school principal."

Leanne shook her head. "No way. He was in Seattle for a conference."

"He could have easily snuck back into town. The

ferry leaves every hour. He could have come back here, stabbed her, then gone back across to Seattle, then left his car at a shop to get the blood out of it."

"Yeah, that's the other thing. We looked at his car."

"No, we didn't."

Leanne tilted her head towards me in question.

"We saw the car he was driving in the parking lot. A car that had a sticker on the back saying 'meat is murder'. And yet, when Gary was making his way to the gym, Kaillie said he was eating some beef jerky."

Leanne gasped. "Oh Saturn, you're right!"

"So he wasn't driving his own car. Probably because his own car was in the shop getting the blood taken out of it."

"And he wouldn't have had it fixed here in town, where it would have been obvious where that much blood would have come from. However, he could have gone to some shady place in the city that wouldn't ask any questions, and still shown up to the conference."

"So who does the car belong to?" Leanne asked, and I shrugged.

"His sister? She seemed like the sort of person who would have a bunch of hippie bumper stickers on the back of her car."

"I guess you're right."

"I'm pretty sure I am. So what do you say, should we go give Detective Andrews what we have?"

"You're joking, right? He's going to laugh us out of there if we tell him all we have to go on is a bumper sticker and a hunch. We need more. We need actual proof."

I groaned. "Don't tell me you think your plan is to go and confront him."

"That's exactly my plan. Come on, it went really well last time."

"You had to save my life when a gun was pulled on me."

"Yeah, almost being the key there. Besides, if the two of us had gone together in the first place things would have gone very differently, since it's harder to shoot two people than just one."

"I'm not one hundred percent sure that logic is sound," I said slowly.

"Oh come on. Gary is a school principal. What's he going to do?"

"Well, he's already stabbed one woman and broken into the coffee shop to try and kill us. I'm pretty sure he's proven that he's willing to resort to violence to get what he wants."

"Fine," Leanne said. "Let's just break into his office and see if there's any proof. Everyone will be gone from the school now, and I know how we can get in without triggering the alarm system."

"How on *earth* would you know that?"

Leanne shrugged. "This is a small town. There's not a lot to do, so we've all climbed up onto the roof of the school at some point or another. There's a skylight up there that we can go through that isn't alarmed. At least, it was still there a couple of years ago."

"Seriously? And no one has thrown paint or anything down it?"

"Oh, that definitely happened. So it's locked now, but you know the spell for unlocking things, right? And we'll be in private, so it's not like there will be anyone around to see us."

I nodded. "I think I can do that." Leanne and Kaillie had been making me use magic to unlock the front door of the house for weeks now, so this was actually one of the spells I was most adept at using. I wasn't worried about messing it up, and I was confident that as long as there was no one else around I'd be fine.

"Cool, let's go," Leanne said. We were going to find proof Gary was the killer.

CHAPTER 24

Fifteen minutes later we'd gotten up onto the roof of the school, with a little bit of help from Leanne for me.

"You know, if you did more yoga you'd have an easier time getting up here," Leanne commented after practically effortlessly making her way onto the roof.

"I'm sure that's a real selling point on the brochure. Break into schools more easily," I puffed, trying to swing my leg over onto the roof while I clutched a pipe attached to the outside wall. Eventually, Leanne was able to grab my leg and pulled it over, and I rolled the rest of my body onto the top of the building. I felt like a seal trying to get onto a rock from the water.

Scratch that. I'd seen seals do that; they were far more elegant than I'd just been.

"Alright," Leanne said, jumping to her feet and making her way to the center of the roof while I got to my feet. She was standing in front of a large skylight that led down into what appeared to be a school hallway. "This is it? Ready?"

I nodded and pulled my wand out from my pocket. I pointed it at the skylight, focused all of my energy on my wand, and thought as hard as I could about the skylight unlocking.

"Saturn, god of freedom, unlock this skylight so that we are welcome."

I grinned as there was an audible click, and a second later Leanne was prying it open. I peered down into the hole. "Well, that looks high."

"It's only like, ten feet or so. Just absorb the landing."

"Easy for you to say," I muttered. "You go first."

"No, you go first. If I go first, you still have the option of wimping out. You could also cast a spell to make a mattress or something down there. Even if things go wrong, we can always text Kaillie to come and fix it."

I strongly considered it. After all, I *had* learned a basic conjuring spell, and I was fairly certain if I dropped into that hole I was going to break both my legs. On the other hand, if things went horribly wrong here and I somehow summoned some demon from the underworld or something, there was no other witch nearby to fix my mistake. It would all be on me.

I thought about what Tina had said, about only

doing magic when I was comfortable. And the more I thought about it, the more I realized I *was* comfortable with this. I had some apprehensions, sure. But I also did know how to cast this spell, there was no risk of any non-magical people seeing it – well, apart from Leanne, but she was allowed to know about magic – and frankly, if I waited until I was perfectly comfortable to cast every spell, I'd probably never cast another one in my life.

"Alright," I said, taking a deep breath and stepping forward, staring into the hole. "Here goes nothing. *Saturn, god of renewal, generate a mattress, that would be super cool.*"

My wand was pointing down into the hole, and a moment later a queen-size mattress appeared, complete with plain white sheets.

"Those are a nice touch, you don't know where the weird magic mattress has been," Leanne said with a grin. "Alright, you're still going first."

I sighed. "Fine. If I die, please give all my stuff to Kaillie."

"Hey," Leanne argued. I grinned at her, held my breath and carefully began lowering myself down the skylight. Eventually I was hanging by my fingertips, I closed my eyes and I let go, squealing the whole way. A second later I landed on the mattress with a soft thud, and rolled off it. I moved all my limbs, and sure enough, there was no pain anywhere.

"All good, your turn," I called up to Leanne, who did

the same as I had. She dropped to the mattress and rolled off elegantly, popping back up to her feet.

"Awesome," she said. "We're in."

I pointed my wand at the mattress. *"Saturn, we're done with this mattress, please return."*

The conjured item immediately disappeared, and I smiled. Magic was still a novelty, and I enjoyed it every time I managed to cast a spell, no matter how simple.

"Alright, let's go," I said, and Leanne led me down the hall toward the principal's office. I had a sneaking suspicion she had been here a few times in her day.

The door was locked, but a quick spell was all that was needed to take care of that, and Leanne and I quickly found ourselves in a room that looked like every other school administrator's office. Cabinets along the wall, a plain desk with a computer, a simple office chair. I imagined there were thousands of offices exactly like this one around the country.

"I'll take the computer, you start looking through the files," Leanne said. "We're looking for anything that might prove he stabbed her, especially letters from Karen telling him she was going to go above his head, or something like that. After all, their dispute was professional."

"Right," I said, nodding. I immediately opened the top part of the file cabinet and began looking through everything Gary had. Most of it was pretty boring, and completely irrelevant to my search, but that was to be expected. After all, as a school principal, he would have had a lot more on his plate than just a dispute with one teacher.

"Find anything?" I asked Leanne after a couple of minutes.

"Not yet. I'm just looking through the email now. Maybe there's something there."

After a couple of minutes, Leanne let out an exclamation. "Here we go!"

I dropped the files I was looking at right back where they belonged – I didn't want Gary to suspect we had been here when he next came in, after all – and headed over to the computer, peering over Leanne's shoulder. She had opened an email from Karen to Gary, dated the morning she was stabbed.

My eyes skimmed over the contents.

Gary,

I'm afraid you're leaving me with no choice but to go to the superintendent in this situation. I respect that our opinions differ, but because this will directly affect the future performance of our students not necessarily on exams but in life, I feel I need to go over your head on this. I can't have my students falling this far behind this early in their education. It's not fair to them, and it's not fair to prevent me from telling their parents the exact nature of the situation. I think we both know the superintendent will be on my side on this, so I urge you to reconsider before I'm forced to take this action. I don't want to take this step, but I strongly believe it is in the best interest of the children I teach, who are my priority.

Regards,

Karen Johnson

"Well, that's a motive if I've ever heard one," I replied.

"There's more, he replied to this," Leanne said, scrolling down. Sure enough, there was a reply from Gary, sent a couple of minutes later.

Karen,

I'm very disappointed to hear you're taking this next step. Could we have a conversation about it? I'm in Seattle for the conference all day, but I can meet you at six, if you'd be willing to come back to the school around then.

Gary

"There's another reply from Karen a few minutes later confirming the appointment," Leanne added. "So they had a meeting scheduled for about an hour before she was stabbed."

"That's crazy!" I said. "Were the emails just sitting there in the account?"

"No," Leanne said, shaking her head. "Gary had deleted all of them. Only, I think he forgot the first rule of the internet: nothing is ever permanently gone. I had to do a bit of tech wizardry, but I got them back."

"I knew you were good with computers, I didn't know you were *this* good."

Leanne smiled at me. "Kaillie grew up getting to do real magic, so I had to find my own magic to do. I pretty quickly realized grown-ups had no idea how computers worked, so I focused a lot of my efforts there. I'm not some Lisbeth Salander-like super hacker, but I know my way around a computer better than most."

"That's cool," I replied, in awe of my cousin. She might have been sensitive about the fact that she had no magical powers, but as far as I was concerned, being able to manipulate computers and find deleted emails like that was just as magical as being able to conjure up a mattress out of nowhere.

"Ok, let me print out these emails, and then we can get out of here and show them to Detective Andrews," Leanne said. The printer whirred to life a moment later, but when I turned to grab them, I gasped.

Standing there in the doorway, his expression one of clouded fury, was Gary Vanderchuk.

CHAPTER 25

"You," I gasped, causing Leanne to turn around as well. "What are you doing here?"

"Do you know how much vandalism has happened to this school because of that skylight? I wanted it sealed up permanently, but the school board refused to pay for that. So when the lock was installed, I also secretly added an alarm. Anytime anyone opened it up I'd get a notification to my phone. So imagine my surprise when I get one such notification tonight."

I sighed. So much for our secret entrance into the school.

"I thought only the other doors were alarmed," Leanne said.

"That's what I wanted everyone to think," Gary replied. "But no, the skylight was as well. It's on a different system, though, because again, the school board wouldn't pay for it. So only I get notified. But in this case, I think that's a good thing. I don't want the cops called in on this."

"Why, because we just found proof that you're the one who tried to kill Karen? And you tried to kill us, too, didn't you? You're the one who broke into the coffee shop and sabotaged all of the wires."

"Yes, that was me," Gary said with a humorless smile. "I'm disappointed that my strategy failed, but I knew I would get away with it. Everyone trusts a high school principal. Meanwhile, Karen's husband was addicted to gambling, and placing bets with Andrew Lloyd, the idiot. He thinks everyone in town is going to keep his secret. Frankly, it's a miracle that he hasn't been turned in by anyone yet. He was the least subtle bookie I have ever met in my life."

"Well, you're not going to get away with it now," Leanne said smugly. "We found the email you sent to Karen and her reply confirming the appointment to meet with you here on the island one hour before she was stabbed."

"Yes, but no one else is going to see it," Gary replied, pulling a gun out from the back of his pants and pointing it at Leanne.

"Oh come on," Leanne said, her voice slightly higher despite the fact that she was trying to act strong. "If you shoot us here, it's going to leave a ton of blood, and no one is going to have any trouble figuring out who killed us."

"That's a good point," Gary said. "Come on, we're going to the supply closet. There's a tarp in there. I'll be able to throw it into the ocean with some rocks and they'll never find your bodies."

Great. This definitely wasn't ideal.

"So you did stab her," Leanne said as Gary motioned for us to move. We both headed to the door. The wand in my pocket felt like an enormous weight. Did I know any spells that I could use against him? Could I even get any spells to work before he noticed and shot me?

Blood pounded through my head. I was panicking. Gary had a gun trained on us and obviously intended to use it. But Leanne was insisting on keeping him talking.

"I did," Gary admitted. "She was going to go to the superintendent. The superintendent here is a loonie leftie hippie type who would have eaten up everything Karen told her. She's hated my guts for years, and I know she's looking for any excuse to have me fired. This is exactly the sort of thing she would have used as ammunition against me. I couldn't let Karen go to her."

"Did you intend to stab her the whole time?" Leanne asked.

"No. I just wanted to talk to her. I wanted to give her one last chance to change her mind, to tell me that she wasn't going to go to the superintendent after all, and that I was right. And I *was* right. After all, the kids who are behind by the time they get to second grade are going to be losers their whole lives. Who cares if they get pushed through a bit, especially if it makes them feel better? They're going to end up being losers anyway, so why bother spending extra time and effort on them when Karen could have concentrated on the kids actually worth teaching."

"Wow, you definitely deserved to be fired," I said, my mouth saying the words before my brain had the time to process what a bad idea it was to say them to a guy with a gun in his hand leading us to our deaths.

"You shut your mouth!" Gary practically screamed at me, waving the gun in my face. "You have *no idea* what it's like dealing with these little jerks every second of every day, while their parents basically just want someone to babysit their kids. Plus, the teachers are just as bad as the students. Don't you dare question me!"

I wisely shut my mouth, fear threatening to over-take me as we walked down the hall. It was kind of eerie, seeing pictures on the walls drawn by obviously-happy young children, full of sunshine and hope while I was being led to my death.

I had to do something. I was the one with magical powers, and if there was any time when it was appro-priate to use them, it had to be now. After all, I couldn't get in trouble for using magic to save my life, could I?

Or Leanne's. Either way, it was a risk I was willing to take.

We had to get out of this.

Eventually, Gary stopped in front of a supply closet. He pulled out a large ring of keys and started looking for the right one, and I knew this was the one chance I was going to have to save my life.

I pulled out the wand and cast one of the first spells I had ever learned, which I muttered under my breath as quietly as I could while I focused as strongly as possible on the gun. "*Saturn, father of Jupiter, take this gun and make it smaller.*"

The gun in Gary's hand began to shrink, and I continued to focus all of my energy towards it, wanting to make it microscopic. Leanne, having noticed what I'd done, rammed into Gary from behind. He shouted, dropping the gun, and I continued to shrink it until it was the size of a quarter.

"What the-?" Gary shouted as he turned, looking for his gun in vain. When he didn't see it, he took a swing at Leanne, but she was too quick. She darted out of the way and kicked him square between the legs, causing Gary to grab at his groin as he groaned in pain. He recovered quickly though, and made a move to attack Leanne, but I screamed and ran at him wildly, with absolutely no idea what I was doing, throwing him off balance just enough that his punch missed my cousin.

Leanne recovered quickly as Gary shoved me away from him and I fell, a squeaking sound reaching my ears as I slid across the floor. She rushed at Gary again, and he punched her square in the face. Blood began streaming from Leanne's nose as I got up to my feet. I rushed towards Gary and kicked him as hard as I could in the knee.

He immediately yelped in pain and grabbed at the joint, the fight forgotten as he collapsed to the ground, howling.

"What have you done? You stupid bitch! You broke my knee!"

"You tried to kill two people, the least you deserve is a little bit of pain," Leanne said, panting, wiping a stray piece of hair from her face.

"What is wrong with you two? How did two small women manage to defeat me?"

Gary continued his rant while Leanne called the authorities, wincing as she kept her nose pinched shut to stop the bleeding. She hung up the phone a minute later and looked at me.

"Detective Andrews should be here in a minute," she said.

"What do I do about the gun?" I asked in a hushed whisper. "Do we pretend it was never here, or do I make it normal-sized again?"

"If you can return it to a regular size I would do that," Leanne said. "There will be fewer questions that way, and Gary will just think he lost sight of it in the heat of the moment."

I nodded and walked away from the two of them,

out of Gary's earshot, and reversed the spell. Gary was now clutching at his knee and crying, his eyes not leaving his leg, so there was no risk he was about to see what would happen. The gun quickly returned to its normal size, and Leanne shot me a thumbs-up sign as she kicked it down the hall, further from the man who was going to kill us with it.

Leanne went to the end of the hall, where a large set of double doors led outside and unlocked them, and about two minutes later Detective Andrews came rushing through them.

"Are you alright?" he asked me immediately, and I nodded.

"I'm fine, yeah."

Then he looked at Leanne, who had blood on the front of her shirt and on her face from when Gary had punched her. "And you? Do you need an ambulance?"

"No," she replied. "But I'm pretty sure this whiny idiot does."

Gary scowled at her while Detective Andrews made the call. When he hung up, he looked at Gary, pulled out a set of handcuffs, and began reading him his rights.

"Gary Vanderchuk, you're under arrest for the attempted murders of Karen Johnson, Eliza Emory and Leanne Stevens. You have the right to remain silent…"

My thoughts trailed off as Detective Andrews finished reading Gary his rights. I couldn't help but realize that he had asked about me – the person who looked relatively unscathed – before Leanne, who had blood all over her face and clothes.

Maybe Leanne was right about him having feelings for me.

I pushed those thoughts from my head as Detective Andrews turned back towards us as Gary continued complaining in the background.

"I want these two arrested! They attacked me! I was just defending the school, they broke in! They're vandals!"

"So, do you two want to tell me exactly what happened here?"

"It depends, are you going to arrest us?" Leanne asked, and Detective Andrews gave her a sly look.

"Do you deserve to be arrested?"

"No. In all honesty, we didn't expect Gary to be here at all, and had no intention of confronting him. If you check your email, you'll find a string of emails between Gary and Karen that I forwarded to you from his office. We intended to leave and then have you arrest him for the murder. But it turns out he had a private alarm set up in the skylight, and he confronted us with a gun. He was taking us to the janitor's closet to get a tarp so he wouldn't make a mess when he killed us."

Detective Andrews sighed. "And I'm sure you just accidentally fell into the skylight, and then decided that while you were here you might as well rifle through the principal's emails."

"That's exactly how it happened. It was totally an accident," I replied.

"Alright, well, I guess that's how I'll have to frame it to the District Attorney," Detective Andrews said. "Now, if you'll excuse me, I think I see some ambulance lights outside, and I need to have a conversation with them about the transport and holding of my prisoner."

CHAPTER 26

The next couple of hours went by as a blur. Gary was taken away by ambulance and transported by ferry to Seattle, since Detective Andrews didn't want Karen to be stressed out by having the man who tried to kill her treated at the same hospital as her. Afterwards, Detective Andrews took us both down to the police station to take our statements. I sat in the waiting area while he spoke to Leanne first, texting Kaillie to let her know we were ok. She had sent about a half dozen texts asking where we were when we didn't come home from yoga class.

When Leanne came out, she winked at me. "Go get 'im, tiger."

"Oh, shut up," I muttered as I made my way into the office and sat down on the chair across from Detective Andrews.

He looked up at me, concern written all over his face. "Are you sure you're alright?"

"I am," I replied. "At least, physically. I'm not totally sure the mental reality has really sunk in yet."

"If you need to see someone, I have some references for a good therapist on the island," Detective Andrews replied. "There's no shame in asking for help if you need it. Mental health is just as important as physical health, and while you might physically be fine, what you've been through was traumatic."

"You sound like someone who knows a lot about this sort of thing, for being a small-island cop."

Detective Andrews smiled, but it was a sad smile. "I did two tours in Iraq after I graduated from high school. I've seen what can happen to people who don't think they need help."

"Ah," I replied. "That explains it. Thank you for the offer. I promise, I will let you know if I need that reference."

"Good," he said. "You're extremely lucky, you know. I can't believe you broke into the school."

"To be fair, we didn't think there was any chance we would get caught."

"But you did get caught, and you were almost killed. Luckily, the two of you were able to overpower him, but it was incredibly risky. He had a gun."

I couldn't correct Detective Andrews and tell him that the gun was already shrinking when Leanne had attacked Gary, and it probably wouldn't have done all that much damage.

"It was fight back, or die," I replied, and he nodded.

"Yes. I'm glad the two of you made that decision, and I'm extremely glad you're both ok. Now, why don't you walk me through exactly what happened."

I spent a good fifteen minutes telling Detective Andrews everything – from having seen the car, realizing it wasn't his, to dropping through the skylight and making it into the office.

"One thing I don't understand is how the two of you managed to get through the hole without hurting yourselves. That's a big drop."

"Oh, I do yoga now, I'm basically an athlete," I replied, earning myself a laugh from Detective Andrews. "Hey! It's not *that* far outside the realm of possibilities. But seriously, we just dangled down from the ledge and absorbed the landing. We probably got a little bit lucky."

"I'll say. Well, I'm glad you're alright." I was just relieved that he accepted that explanation and I wasn't going to have to come up with an even bigger lie. After all, I couldn't exactly tell him I had magically conjured up a mattress that we jumped down onto. "I think given the extenuating circumstances the two of you aren't going to get into any trouble for breaking into the school. But I will warn you again – please stay out of any future crimes. This is the second time since you've moved here that you almost died. I'd really appreciate it if it didn't happen again."

"Don't worry," I said with a small smile. "I don't want it to happen again, either, Detective."

"Good," he said, and I stood up to go. "One second," he said, and I stopped, turning to look at him. Detective Andrews bit his lip, like he was trying to decide on something, and then finally said it. "Listen, Eliza. Would you like to go out with me? For dinner? If you say yes, you might want to start calling me Ross, instead of Detective."

"Yes," I replied, the word having left my mouth before I'd had a second to fully consider it. "That sounds great."

That sounds great? What was wrong with me? It wasn't that I didn't like Detective – erm, Ross – it was that I wasn't really looking for a relationship right now. Or ever, really. And yet, one flash of that smile that made dimples appear in his cheeks and I'd collapsed like a house of cards in the wind.

On the bright side, it wasn't like Ross was a bad guy. Actually, I did like him, when he wasn't warning me to stay out of investigations I had no business sticking my nose into. And I supposed I couldn't really blame him for that.

"Awesome," he said. "I'm working tomorrow night, but how about the night after that?"

"Sure," I said with a smile. Actually, the more I thought about it, the more I was ok with it. Who knew?

Maybe it would be fun. It had been a long time since I had been on a date, but I probably wouldn't embarrass myself too badly.

"Great. I'll see you then."

"Yeah, sure thing," I replied, getting up from the chair and making my way back out into the lobby, where Leanne was waiting for me.

"What's up with you?" she asked.

"What do you mean?"

"Your face is so red it's like someone went to town with fire engine paint on your face."

"Oh no," I replied, my hands rushing to my cheeks. They were definitely warm.

Leanne grinned. "So what happened?"

"He, uh, kind of asked me out," I replied, and felt my face go an even deeper shade of red.

"I knew it!" Leanne barked out with a celebratory fist-pump. "So when's the date? You did say yes, didn't you? You better have said yes."

"I said yes," I admitted. "It's the day after tomorrow. You're going to have to help me figure out what to wear. I haven't been on a date in so long, I'm kind of nervous."

"Oh don't you worry about that. I've got you," Leanne said, wrapping an arm around my shoulders and leading me out of the police station.

✴

*O*ver the next day or so, the rumor mill began swirling, and we found out quite a bit at the coffee shop about what was going on in town.

Gary Vanderchuck admitted to everything in exchange for a plea deal that would have him spend the next fifteen years in jail. He had been at the conference, rushed back to meet with Karen, and stabbed her in his car. He then drove back to Seattle via the ferry and took the car to a shady place that didn't ask too many questions about replacing the upholstery before making his way back to the hotel bar, so that enough people noted his presence that he still had a decent alibi.

Andrew Lloyd went to the police station first thing the next morning and also admitted to everything he had done. Apparently, the guilt really was too much for him and he wanted to own up to everything. It also turned out he had donated all of his ill-gotten money to various charities on the island and in other parts of Washington State. The rumor was a plea deal was going to be made with him given his honesty, and he would be treated leniently.

Karen, for her part, was making a miraculous recovery now that she was back home. We even heard she was scheduled to be discharged in just a couple of days. I was thrilled for her, and for her family. I didn't know if she was still going to go ahead with the divorce, but for now, she was home, and she was safe.

Aunt Lucywas annoyed that she didn't get to be involved in the final takedown, and made sure we knew it when we went to eat dinner the following night at Aunt Debbie's place, with none of us wanting to cook after a long day at the coffee shop.

"I can't believe you didn't invite me along," she said, shaking her head. "Do you know how useful I am in these types of situations?"

"You would have broken a hip jumping through the skylight," Leanne protested. "We couldn't bring you."

"Be careful, I can and will hex you," Aunt Lucy replied, pulling out her wand and waving it threateningly at Leanne.

"It wasn't supposed to be an adventure anyway," I said. "We were just supposed to go in, find proof Gary had done it, and get out. And we found the proof. It was good thinking by you to forward it on to Ross. That way, no matter what happened to us, he still would have found the killer."

"I've seen way too many TV shows where people sit on information and it ends up biting them in the rear," Leanne replied. "I wasn't about to let that happen to us. By the way... Ross?"

"Yeah, well, I can't really call him Detective Andrews anymore, can I?" I muttered, embarrassed.

"Oooh, yes, less than twenty-four hours before the big date," Kaillie grinned. "Are you excited?"

"I'm excited to stop talking about it right now," I said.

"Someone's testy," Aunt Lucy said, helping herself to another pork chop.

"Well I think it's nice that Eliza is settling in so well here," Aunt Debbie added. "And you should leave her and her private life alone."

"Yeah," I said, glaring at the others.

"That said, I do wish you'd all be more careful. You're my nieces, and I don't want to see you in danger, and yet that's exactly what happened the other day."

"Again, we were breaking and entering, we didn't expect to face off against a killer," Leanne sighed, exasperated.

"Well, next time you're committing a crime – even if it's just a misdemeanor – I want an invite," Aunt Lucy said.

"No, she doesn't," Aunt Debbie said, glaring at her sister. "Especially because there isn't going to be a next time. You girls are going to stay on the right side of the law, right?"

"Of course we are," Kaillie said, nodding enthusiastically. "You can count on us, Mom."

I smiled as I looked around the table. These people were my family, and I couldn't be happier. I was getting used to life here on Enchanted Enclave, and I couldn't wait to see what the future had in store for me.

*B*ook 3: **A Witch, Dark Roast:** When another body pops up at a new construction site in Enchanted Enclave, Eliza doesn't want to have anything to do with the investigation. After all, she's had a few close calls, and Detective Andrews warned her not to get involved in police matters in the future.

However, as more information comes out, there seems to be something strange afoot. When it becomes obvious that there's a paranormal hiding in their midst, Eliza and her cousins decide they need to get involved, not only for justice sake, but to keep the residents of Enchanted Enclave safe. But being so isolated from the paranormal world, they find themselves at a disadvantage.

Between finding the killer, trying to figure out why Aunt Lucy has been acting so secretive and dealing with some chaos at the coffee shop, Eliza has a lot of balls in the air. Will she be able to solve all of her problems before everything comes crashing down around her?

Click or tap here to read A Witch, Dark Roast now.

ALSO BY SAMANTHA SILVER

Thank you so much for reading! Here's how to keep up with my books in this series and others:

- Sign up for my newsletter to be the first to find out about new releases, and get a free bonus novella from the Western Woods series: http://www. samanthasilverwrites.com/newsletter

- You can also check out the next book in this series, Whole Latte Magic, by clicking here: http://www. samanthasilverwrites.com/awitchdarkroast

If you enjoyed the visit from the Western Woods witches, they have their own series! You can read all about Tina and friends' adventures here:

Back to Spell One (Book 1)

Two Peas in a Potion (Book 2)

Three's a Coven (Book 3)

Four Leaf Clovers (Book 4)

Five Charm Fire (Book 5)

Six Ways to Spellday (Book 6)

Seven Year Witch (Book 7)

Behind the Eight Spell (Book 8)

Or you can discover any of the other series I write by clicking the links below:

Pacific North Witches Mysteries

Pacific Cove Mysteries

Willow Bay Witches Mysteries

Magical Bookshop Mysteries

California Witching Mysteries

Cassie Coburn Mysteries

Ruby Bay Mysteries

ABOUT THE AUTHOR

Samantha Silver lives in British Columbia, Canada, along with her husband and a little old doggie named Terra. She loves animals, skiing and of course, writing cozy mysteries.

å

You can connect with Samantha online here:

Facebook

Email

For the most up-to-date info and lots of goodies like sneak previews, cover reveals and more, join my Facebook Reader Group by clicking here.

Printed in Great Britain
by Amazon